P9-EJY-909

THE WORLD
BENEATH

Also by Aaron Gwyn

DOG ON THE CROSS: STORIES

AARON GWYN

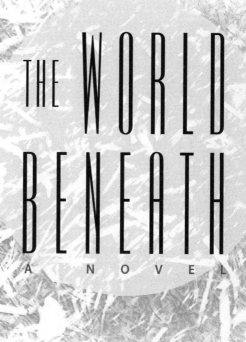

THE WORLD BENEATH

A NOVEL

W. W. NORTON & COMPANY / NEW YORK LONDON

For information about permission to reproduce selections from this book,
write to Permissions, W. W. Norton & Company, Inc.,
500 Fifth Avenue, New York, NY 10110

For information about special discounts for bulk purchases, please contact
W. W. Norton Special Sales at specialsales@wwnorton.com or 800-233-4830

Manufacturing by Courier Westford
Book design by Ellen Cipriano
Production manager: Anna Oler

Library of Congress Cataloging-in-Publication Data

Gwyn, Aaron.
The world beneath : a novel / Aaron Gwyn.
p. cm.
ISBN 978-0-393-06723-1
1. Missing persons—Investigation—Fiction. 2. Sheriffs—Fiction.
3. Persian Gulf War, 1991—Veterans—Fiction. 4. Oklahoma—Fiction.
5. Psychological fiction. I. Title.
PS3607.W96W67 2009
813'.6—dc22   2008052427

W. W. Norton & Company, Inc.
500 Fifth Avenue, New York, N.Y. 10110
www.wwnorton.com

W. W. Norton & Company Ltd.
Castle House, 75/76 Wells Street, London W1T 3QT

1 2 3 4 5 6 7 8 9 0

for Lance Corporal Scott Sparks—
and my grandfather,

J.L.M.

There was the sense—an almost religious conviction—among many of the Plains Indians that something malevolent traveled beneath them. This was more than a malign, abstract force. It was a presence, a person, a character as fully developed in the Native American psyche as the Satan of Hebraic writings or those demons who assailed Buddha during his trial of Enlightenment.

Enoch Malcoz,
Deep Dweller: Stories of America's First Man

THE WORLD
BENEATH

PROLOGUE

He closed the passenger door and followed the two of them down the trail. Just a narrow path through the oak trees, thick branches, thickly leaved. It was summer and hot. The leaves drawn into themselves. They had the look of shriveled hands. The air on his face felt humid, thick, and though he'd just exited the Camaro, he'd already begun to sweat. There was perspiration on his shoulders. Perspiration on his face. He thought he'd say something about it, but Herring would only mock him. Better, as always, to keep it quiet.

He was good at this, keeping quiet. Around Herring he had to be. And now even around Charles. At one time it was just the two of them—J.T., Charles—but they were fifteen now and there was the issue of cars. Women. Suddenly, a hundred other things. Christopher Herring would turn seventeen that August and he'd been driving since the age of twelve. J.T. didn't like him, but he was friends now with Charles. Which meant he'd have to be his as well.

He followed them, keeping himself a few paces back. Charles was laughing. Trying to make Herring laugh. It'd become that way. Herring was white and Charles was black and J.T. thought of himself as neither. His mother had been Latina. His father, Chickasaw.

Both were gone now.

Sounded like neither to him.

The trail made a turn and then it made another. The dirt was red and soft as a powder. In other places, hard and baked. You'd see, time to time, hoofprints where cows had crossed, the U's on the ground like impressions in plaster. The path went uphill, swung to the left, then began sloping down. J.T. stepped carefully. Ahead of him, Charles laughed at something, said something about church. It was the only word J.T. caught. That and *carpet*. Was he talking, J.T. wondered, about the church where he used to go?

"Fuck the church," Herring said.

The trail began to widen and he heard the shush of water. They were trying to strike the creek below the falls. Herring said this path would take them to it. He'd been high since noon and he said a lot of things. Driving out, he'd kept passing the joint to the backseat and J.T. would hold the smoke in his cheeks, blow it quickly out. He was fairly sure Charles had been doing the same. He'd begun thinking otherwise when they emerged into a clearing and crested out upon a bluff. The stream wound beneath them, gradually narrowed, rushed over a sandstone lip. It made a falls into the pool below. J.T. had heard people talk about it. The drop and the water. No telling how deep. There was a bank around the pool where the ground fell sheer. At the other end, an opening where the stream flowed out. Trees flanked the water, giving that sense of enclosure. J.T. wondered: Was it an *inlet* or a *nook*? Perhaps even a *cove*. He thought *cove*, and then *alcove*, trying to decide which was better, unable to decide.

A massive pecan stood beside the stream, one of its larger limbs stretched above them, and then out above the pool. Someone had attached a length of cable. Maybe twenty feet or so of cable, thin and black with a loop at its end, knots spaced every few inches. It hung above the pool like a rigid noose. Herring gestured to it and the three boys stood staring. Too high to use as a swing into the water. Only purpose would be dangling out there, tempting your fate. They talked about this a few minutes and then Charles turned, sunlight glancing off his spectacles. He went over and picked up a branch. He brought it back, handed it to Herring, and they took turns trying to hook the cable and bring it within reach. J.T. watched for a moment, then went over and seated himself on a stone. He wiped the sweat from his neck, braced his arms upon his knees.

He felt, of a sudden, very tired and he thought that he could maybe sleep. He wasn't getting enough, his nana told him. His aunt told him this as well. Charles and Herring's chatter drifted to the background, and J.T. sat listening to the water as it sluiced through the stone channel and splashed into the pond. It sounded like someone saying, *Shhhhhhhhhhhhhhhhhhhhhhhhhhhhhhhhhh.*

His eyes had just closed when Charles asked him something. He opened them. Indicated he hadn't heard.

"Tonight," Charles repeated. "You still staying over?"

J.T. said he couldn't. In the morning he had to work.

"Work," said Charles.

"Fuck work," Herring said.

The two of them had managed, by this point, to retrieve the cable and were leaning back, tugging on it, first one, then the other, testing the line, trying to determine its strength. Herring said it would hold them, but Charlie wasn't sure.

"There's metal inside it. It's like it's full of rust."

Herring pulled on it. On his right forearm was the tattoo he'd gotten from a parlor down in Dallas. *Ramrod*, the letters read. No one called him this but Charlie. Herring was tall and thin, his blond hair shaved into a narrow crew. He wore a sleeveless T-shirt. Blue jeans. Boots. Charlie wore the same, trying to copy him, J.T.

thought. He'd even shaved his head. But Charlie was much smarter. Charlie was so much kinder.

"What are you?" Charles asked. "One seventy? One seventy-five?"

"One fifty-eight," said Herring.

"Yeah," said Charles. "We'd snap it for sure."

Herring stood there a moment.

Looked at J.T.

Said it would definitely hold him.

J.T. knew what was coming. He was too tired to even fuss. On the scales at the golf course he weighed one twenty-five. He worked the greens at the course, and he snuck, on occasion, to the club-house, went down the hallway to the lockers. He'd hoped to put on weight, but he couldn't seem to do that, and the metal ruler atop the scale marked him at sixty-five inches. This was in sneakers. He was fifteen years old and he'd grown all that he would.

He stood from the rock and brushed the seat of his pants. He walked over and took the cable in his grip.

"It'll break," warned Charlie.

Herring said it wouldn't.

"Why won't it?"

"It's cable," Herring said.

J.T. didn't think about it. You had to do these things. Boy of his stature, you had to do them all the time. Jump this, swing off that, you got used to it. You broke ankles, chipped teeth, but this was the price you paid for belonging, and there was very little belonging left.

And so you took what you could, which was now a length of cable in black insulation, the plastic peeling to where you saw the metal beneath. J.T. didn't test it. He didn't even try. He planted a foot in the stirrup, took a step back, and, holding the cable tightly, launched himself above the pool. He swung out with the breeze gone

suddenly cool, light glancing off the water, and he'd just reached the
end of the cable's arc, started back toward the bank, when the tension went slack, and he looked to see the cable snap an inch above his
grip. His stomach shrank inside him. His throat tightened shut. He
was suspended in the air a moment and then began to fall. The pool
rushing toward him, his body twisting prone. He was almost flat
when he struck the water. It nearly took his breath.

Then he was swimming, moving quickly through the water,
almost, it seemed, upon it, noise coming from the bank above him,
from Herring and Charles. And then he was out, slipping on stones
at the edge of the pool, and then scrambling up the side of the
bank, hands pulling at him, standing there beside Charles, panting
and drenched. His heart pounded in his head. Adrenaline buzzing. He could've hit a submerged rock or tree stump. He could've
broken his back.

"Holy shit!" Charles was saying. "Holy shit!"

J.T. looked at Herring. He knew better than to speak.

"You all right?" said Charles.

He nodded.

"You okay?"

He nodded again.

"Holy shit!" said Charles, face beaming wonder.

Herring seemed disappointed that he wasn't hurt.

"It was like something off the TV," said Charles.

J.T. shook his head.

"Like the TV," said Charles. He glanced at Herring. "Was that
not like TV? Was that not the shit?"

"Fuck the TV," Herring said.

It was close to midnight when he came up the drive. He walked across
the lawn to the chanting of crickets and went through the back

door, up the back stairs, to the kitchen. The lights were out, but there was the glare of a lamp from the living room. He could see its reflection on the kitchen tiles. He took off his sneakers and laid them out upon a towel. He peeled his socks off, left them to dry as well. He stood for a moment, watching the moon out the window, light filtering through the leaves. A sick sea-light. The incessant swirl of insects. He turned and stepped over and went across the floor, leaving footprints of vapor that vanished as he passed.

In the living room, his grandmother was seated in her uphol-stered rocker, black and yellow paisley, passed on by her mother. She was asleep now, glasses low on her nose and her Spanish Bible parted upon her breast. She was a thin woman, very small, and, sleeping, she resembled, almost, a child. Her wrinkles smoothed out. Her hair was thick. She'd continued, all these years, to dye it. Coils of velvet black. He stood looking down on her, swallowing it back. He whispered her name, though he knew she wouldn't hear. He said it low enough she couldn't. The book on her chest rose and fell. Rose and fell. She was wearing a white flannel nightgown, even for all the heat, and her feet were encased in slippers he'd bought her the previous winter.

He stood several minutes, watching the slack expression on her face. He leaned closer, careful, like kneeling before a shrine. Beneath lids the consistency of paper, you could just make out her eyes, a pair of marbles covered by parchment. Every so often they would twitch. The boy wondered what she dreamt of. And did she worry in her dreams? He inhaled, gently released the breath. A shudder passed through him and he thought, for some reason, this was the last he would see of her. A panicked thought. He was used to it. This woman, a last link to ancestors he vaguely imagined. His love for her like an iron upon his chest. He touched the fingers of his right hand to his lips. He started to move the Bible, but that would only wake her. Gingerly, he took a crocheted blanket from the back of the rocker, and then knelt there, tucking it around her slippered feet. He stood for several moments, and then went up the stairs.

In his room, he sat at the small desk. The house was quiet. Stale and hot. There was a fan on the shelf that oscillated back and forth. He sat there with the dictionary open before him, thumbing pages, thumbing more. He looked up *cove* and *alcove*. He looked up *nook*, *inlet*, and *bay*. He read the definitions and next to each he made a dot with the lead of his pencil. He closed the dictionary and put it back in its place and then he sat there, thinking of Charles. Of Nana. His aunt. He could feel them all receding.

He turned off the lamp and stepped over and lay upon his bed. Atop the covers of his bed. The room was dark. Blackout blinds over his window. He lay there in his boxer shorts with the air moving across his legs, prickling them slightly. He could just feel the breath of the fan, then the absence of the breath when it turned away. He stayed like this, perfectly still, and when he could take it no longer rolled onto his side, sat at the edge of the mattress, then turned and knelt on the floor.

He braced his elbows against the bed. He clasped together his hands. He crossed ankles, left over right, rubbed the arch of one foot against the heel of the other, then recrossed his ankles, right over left. He prayed the words that ran inside him. Four words. Over and over. He clenched his eyes tightly and after a few moments he could see a light on the inside of the lids like the negative of a picture, two light holes swimming in black. He tried to focus on this. He focused on the words. He repeated them again and again and then broke into the slightest whisper. He pressed his lips to the blanket and muttered into his quilt.

"Let me be taken," he said. "Let me be taken. Let me be taken. Let me be taken."

Sheriff Martin turned into the parking lot and pulled into the handicapped place just in front of the building. It was early evening, cold November, and there was a line extending out the door, onto the sidewalk, over in front of the law offices of Sokolove and Phelps. Retired couples. Teenagers. Single men in their thirties, standing huddled in on themselves, staring at their feet. The sign atop the building read *Ernie's Soft-Serve & Yogurt*, and the GRAND OPENING banner still hung across the plate-glass window. Martin sat watching a moment, then reached for the door handle. As he did, the radio coughed his call sign, then went silent, then coughed again. He was waiting for the third time when he unhooked the receiver and brought it to his mouth.

"County One," he said.

"Sheriff?"

"Go ahead, Nita."

"Sheriff?"

"Yeah, Nita. Right here."

"I'm sorry," the woman told him. "I couldn't get ahold of Lem."

"It's all right."

"I don't think his unit's working."

"It's okay, Nita. What do you need?"

There was a pause. Martin looked out the windshield and watched an elderly man emerge from Ernie's with a small Styrofoam bowl. The man stood on the sidewalk and began spooning the bowl's contents to his mouth. His breath was fogging from the cold, and his ears turned a bright shade of red, but he kept eating regardless.

"We had a call come in," said Nita, "out on 99. On past the four-mile, two miles back east."

"Out by Grainger's?"

"Yeah," said Nita. "Spanish lady. Her daughter made the call. She hasn't seen her grandson in a couple days."

"How many days?"

"Two or three."

"How old's the boy?"

"Says he just turned fifteen. He was supposed to be with friends, but the friends' parents don't know nothing about it."

Martin sat a moment. The man was still there on the sidewalk. He spooned a final bite into his mouth and then stood studying the bowl. He tossed it in a nearby trash can, walked down, and stepped back into line.

"You want me to wait, get ahold of Lem?"

"No," said Martin, "I'll take it."

"You sure? Probably a mix-up."

"Yeah, I'm sure. You mind calling Deb?"

"She expecting you?"

"She is," said Martin. "And, Nita?"

"Sheriff?"

"You find Lem, send him down to Ernie's. Tell him one scoop vanilla, one scoop chocolate. No nuts. Have him run it out to the house."

There was another pause. Martin imagined the woman writing. She said, "One scoop vanilla, one scoop chocolate."

"No nuts."

"Got it," she said. "No nuts."

Martin started the engine and shifted into reverse. "Thanks, Nita. Tell Lem I said thanks."

The woman chuckled. "It's ice cream now, is it, Sheriff?"

"Yeah," said Martin. "Ice cream and everything else."

He drove out 99 past the city limits and airstrip, the construction supply companies, the local plant farm and nursery. It was dark now and clear and Martin would duck his head from time to time and glance at stars. Orion to one side. Over there the Dipper. He could see Cassiopeia's W etched sideways above his rearview mirror, its lowest line slanting down. Martin had spent three years in his early thirties working a fire-watch tower in the mountains of southern Colorado, and since being back he'd come to appreciate the open feeling, the wideness of sky. He'd known easterners who'd come west from Knoxville and Atlanta, and when they hit the broad expanse of Oklahoma prairie they cowed under that sense of infinite horizon. Martin drove a mile under the speed limit with the scanner dialed down and the radio's volume turned a little higher. He glanced over and saw the moon was two days till full and just beginning to rise.

A few miles outside town, he turned onto a narrow blacktop that took him back to the east. He passed brick homes on one-acre properties, their driveways done with white shell and gravel, and then he passed the drives to oil leases, the occasional farm.

There were fields of winter wheat and cattle, and then the woods thickened and there were dense stands of blackjack and pine. The blacktop changed to gravel and then to red dirt, and the limbs of the oaks stretched above him, making of the road a tunnel or arch. Things were different out here. The people were different. They had the feeling of another time.

Martin slowed and began checking the numbered stakes that had been hammered alongside mailboxes, two or three per mile. The county had just implemented a 911 program, and workers had to assign each residence a number. He passed *1302* and *1303* and then he drove down farther and the next stake he saw read *1305*. He pulled into a driveway, backed out, and began going back the way he'd come.

He saw the marker this time on the north edge of the road. The drive was dirt and the mailbox alongside it was just an aluminum rectangle and a length of two-by-four driven into the ground. No flag. *Fuentes* lettered across it in a back-slanted scrawl. He pulled in and went slowly back into the trees, two ruts worn by tires and between them a thatch of dead weeds. There were brambles and sumac bushes standing high on both sides of the drive. There were potholes he'd come up on quickly and have to jerk the wheel to dodge.

A quarter mile down he emerged into a clearing and saw the house. It was a dark two-story, covered in sandstone and mortar. A Canadian Valley yard light was mounted high atop an electrical pole and it bathed everything in an acetylene glow. The dirt drive made a circle in front of the residence and he pulled around it and turned off the engine. He checked in with Nita, confirmed location, and then he just sat. Up on the second floor, the windows blushed yellow against their blinds. Trees surrounded the home. Their branches fingered its eaves and awning. On the front stoop a calico watched him from slanted eyes. Martin took a notepad from an overhead cubby and placed it in the pocket of his shirt. He tripped the door handle and got out. He stepped a few feet from the cruiser and then he stepped back. He opened the door, reached in, and fetched his radio. He shook his head. Since Deborah's pregnancy, he often found himself forgetting. It was a matter of anticipation, nerves, and it violated Martin's principal rule. Negligence was an extreme thing.

There was a row of sandstone steps leading up to the door, twenty of them, twenty-two. They were worn at their center, beveled at the edge. Martin walked up and rapped twice with a knuckle. He waited a moment, knocked again. He could hear muffled voices that might have been a television, though he'd seen no antenna on the house, no satellite or dish. He lifted a hand to knock a third time and the door opened and there was a Latina woman standing on a woven cloth rug, clutching to her shoulder a very young child. She nodded to Martin and motioned him inside.

He followed her through a foyer and into the living room. He followed her up a flight of carpeted stairs, past rows of photographs, across a landing, and down a hall. It was cold in the house and the walls were paneled in cedar. Everything seemed to carry that smell. At the last door on the left, the young woman stopped. She shifted her child to the other arm, tapped the doorframe, and muttered something in Spanish. Then she opened the door and looked back at Martin.

"This is Nana," she said.

It was a small room, immaculately kept, and inside it was an antique dresser and rocker and a king-sized bed with a canopy and spiral-carved posts. It made the room seem smaller than it was. On the edge of the bed sat an elderly matron in a polyester dress, black hair pinned atop her head in an intricate bun. She was a thin woman, very short. Her feet barely brushed the floor. She had a handkerchief clutched in one hand and she was rocking slightly, shaking her head. The young woman went over and said something once again in Spanish. She spoke softly, and pointed at Martin, but the old woman looked at the floor.

Martin placed his hat atop the dresser and pulled the tablet from his shirt pocket. He removed his pen and gave it a click.

At this, the elderly woman looked up. She blinked several times and then began to speak. As she talked, her voice pitched higher. She spoke faster and faster, the words liquid, aggrieved.

Martin waved briefly the pen and tablet. He told her he couldn't understand.

"No comprende," he said. "No habla Español."

The young woman reached and placed a hand on her mother's shoulder. She said something in a low voice, and then she said, "Shhhhhhhhhhh."

Martin stood there feeling awkward. Like a man broken in on a lovers' quarrel or brawl.

"What," he heard himself asking, "is your name?"

"Angelica," the young woman said.

"*An-hey-lee-ka*," said Martin, writing.

She palmed the back of the child's head. Stroked it. The baby watched Martin with widened eyes.

"Your mother's upset," he said.

"Yes."

"She gets like this?"

The woman nodded.

Martin smiled. He motioned for her to go on.

Angelica glanced at her mother, and then back at Martin. She lowered her voice to a whisper and said, "It's Thomas."

Thomas, Martin wrote.

"He's Nana's grandson. We haven't seen him. It's been since Thursday night."

Martin wrote, *Thursday*.

"Where are his parents?" he asked.

Angelica shook her head. She removed her hand from her mother's shoulder and made an ambiguous gesture.

Martin wrote.

"About how old?" he asked.

"He turned fifteen in June."

"What's his school?"

"He doesn't go."

"He doesn't go to school?"

"No," Angelica told him, "he works at the course."

"The golf course?"

"He helps with the greens."

Martin wrote this as well. He smoothed a hand across his chin. He asked the woman could she give a description.

Angelica sat there a moment. She leaned over and whispered something to her mother. Her mother nodded. She blotted her eyes with the handkerchief, then climbed from the bedside, walked to the bureau, opened the drawer, and began shuffling through it. She took up something and turned and handed it to her daughter. The way you might present a thing made of glass. Angelica walked to Martin so he could see.

It was an eight-by-five photograph, probably done for school. The picture was a headshot, cropped at the shoulders, but you could tell the boy was small for his age. He had dark hair and eyes. Fine features. Light brown skin. He was wearing a white T-shirt and he was smiling broadly.

Martin studied the boy. His eyebrows and face. He looked at Angelica and tapped the photo against his chest. The aunt nodded and he slipped it inside his shirt pocket.

"How long ago was it taken?"

Angelica told him last year.

"He look any different?"

"No."

"How tall?"

"Five-four," said Angelica. "Five-five."

"About what would you say—hundred-twenty, hundred-thirty pounds?"

"Maybe."

"He goes by *Thomas?*"

"No," said the woman. "He goes by 'J.T.' "

"J.T.?"

"Yes."

"What's his last name?"

Angelica shook her head.

"His last name," said Martin, rolling a hand in the air. "His *name* name."

"Fuentes," she said. "Javier Thomas. His father was a Harjo. He goes by our name now."

Martin wrote this on his pad. He asked what the boy was wearing when she'd seen him last. Angelica turned and asked her mother and at this the elderly woman began to weep. She went over and sat on the edge of her bed. She rocked slightly back and forth and smoothed her dress across her lap. Angelica told her not to cry. She said, "Shhhhhh, Nana," but the woman didn't stop. Her voice was coming louder and her shoulders shook. Martin stood watching. He wanted to say something, but it just felt wrong. He shifted his weight from foot to foot, stared down at the pad. Then he nodded to Angelica, picked his hat off the dresser, walked out of the room, and closed the door behind him. He went down the hallway toward the stairs. One of the doors he passed was cracked several inches and a light came from just inside. Martin stopped and pushed it back on its hinge.

It was the boy's room. There were pairs of sneakers in a row by the dresser. A small bed. A bedside table with a banker's lamp and pull chain. The walls were covered in magazine clippings. The ceiling as well. One vast collage. Martin stepped in to better see. Clippings of golfers, equipment; of courses, sand traps, flags. There was a poster above the headboard of an oversized hole, shot from inside looking up—a circle of blue, and at one edge, the shadow of a ball on the cusp of the rim, ready to eclipse the ring of cloudless sky.

Martin studied it for several minutes. He thought it must have taken years. He walked over to the wall and brushed his hand across its surface. There was a plywood table there serving as a desk. A lamp and a coffee cup of pencils. A dictionary balanced on end. It was an old dictionary, dog-eared, a hundred markers jutting from its pages. Martin opened it. He began to flip through. There were checkmarks beside words, some pages filled with checkmarks, definitions underlined. He went from the front of the book to its back. Then he sat it on the desk and went downstairs.

On his drive back to the station, he rehearsed what Angelica had said. Once she'd calmed her mother and come back down to talk. She told how her nephew had fallen in with a rougher crowd. How his friends were older, larger, and Thomas wanted so badly to impress. He was a good boy, she said. It was his circumstance. No car, no money. It was being half Chickasaw, half Latino, always in between.

"He doesn't have nothing," said Angelica. "All he got is us."

Martin took down the names of J.T.'s friends. One of them he knew. Christopher Herring. He'd had to call his parents one time, issue a warning. And he thought what Angelica told him was true. Perser was a dying town. Sixty-nine hundred people. It had boomed to thirty thousand back in the twenties, but then the petroleum market fell and the jobs along with it. The only industries were the oil patch and a factory outside the city limits that made blue jeans and boots.

It was easy to see why a teen might run from that.

Harder for Martin to see how he could not.

It was after midnight when he unlocked the front door, stepped quietly inside, and hung his keys on the peg. The hallway flickered with a cool electric light. Martin took off his boots and placed them on the tile next to Debbie's. He walked onto the carpet in his socked feet and rounded the corner into the living room. The television was on and the sound was muted and Deborah lay stretched in her recliner. She had two blankets, but she'd kicked them off in her sleep, and her T-shirt was pulled up, exposing her stomach. Beside the chair, on the craft tray, her newest model—this one an F-4 Phantom she'd painted camouflage and gray. Martin could see she'd finished the cockpit that evening, begun applying decals, final touches of paint. It looked, to him, very good.

He picked up her sweatshirt from the floor and draped it over the back of a chair. He stood there, watching her sleep. She had black marks on her fingers from where she missed with the brush, black marks on her chin. Martin doubted she'd even notice. Some women would not have liked it, but Debbie, she was more concerned with the planes. She'd served in the Navy aboard an aircraft carrier during Desert Storm, and in the third month of her pregnancy she'd begun to build models and hang them in the baby's room. There was the F-4 and an A-6 Intruder. An F-14. A tank-killer with a fifty-caliber gun, though Martin couldn't recall its name. They dangled around the crib from pieces of fishing line, an entire squadron. She'd done two models in the past week, sitting in her chair eating ice cream and watching movies on HBO. Martin saw a stack of Styrofoam bowls on the coffee table. He smiled to himself and leaned down to kiss her navel, which had just begun to pucker and point. He found the remote next to a row of model kits from her most recent trip to the store. Martin tried to buy them for her, but he only got the wrong ones. He once bought her a kit for a commercial aircraft by mistake. It was a 747 and Debbie wasn't interested enough to even take it from its wrapping. She only gave him a kind look and shook her head.

"I don't like it if it doesn't shoot," she said.

He woke in the night from a dream he could not recall and sat up in bed with a start. There was no light in the house and he could hear his wife sleeping beside him, the rise and fall of her breath. Martin rubbed his eyes. It was warm in their room and he was sweating. His T-shirt was soaked. He struggled out of the garment and let it fall to the floor and then he sat there, studying his feet. In his dream, something had been threatened, but he couldn't remember what. He still had the feeling, though. Used to be, it was with him all the time. About his brother. Martin had lost him very young. He sat there, thinking. An image of willow leaves and cicadas and morning on the Arkansas River. Pete's head disappearing beneath the surface. The sheriff marveled. He hadn't pictured it in quite a while.

He took a clean shirt from the drawer in the nightstand and slipped it over his head. Their bedroom window looked onto the east side of the property, down through the oak grove toward the pond. You could see water now the leaves had fallen. The reflection of moonlight. He lay back against the mattress and thought about the boy and it seemed the creep of something was out there in the dark. He started to get up and go down the hallway, but then he reached out and placed his hand on Deborah and found her stomach. He touched it lightly, not wanting to wake her. Beneath that layer of skin and fluid, his son. He'd seen his ghost image on the sonogram two weeks before. Martin thought about that. He leaned and placed his ear very close. He'd do that sometimes. Lean over while she was sleeping and listen. His first marriage had ended with a stillborn boy. Martin moved closer. He listened for a while and tried to recall his dream. Deborah stirred and mumbled something, but he didn't understand. He meant to turn and ask her, and then he was asleep.

THOMAS SPEAKS

I had this feeling then my father was underground. I don't know why, exactly. I think because of Nana. Something she said. I think when I first asked she told me this thing in Spanish. I can see her talking: her lips dry and her eyes moist, her mouth, when it moved, like the jawbone on a dummy. Hair dyed black. Norteño skin. She smoothed her palms across her lap and called me Thomas. I could smell her perfume. My love for her was a fierce, hurting love. That was how she taught me. She pulled me close and said my name and pressed me against her. She is a small woman, but she can seem so large. She spoke of my father and his death. And the way she said it, I knew it was to make it softer. Try and make it right. She didn't want to say he was dead, exactly. She didn't want to say buried.

And so he was subterráneo, she told me.

Underground.

The truth is he died in prison. It was after Mama passed. He was out West working a pipeline and he was accomplice in a triple murder. I don't know what they mean, "accomplice." If it maybe means he helped. He went to prison, though, and he had diabetes, and he went into shock one morning, and that afternoon he died. I was a baby. Nana says we got a letter and his belt buckle and a check for one hundred thirty dollars. I never knew what for.

When I was five I came home and asked Aunt Angelica. I didn't know what a father was. I thought he was something to do with school. She was standing at the counter, slicing tomatoes for supper, and I asked her, and she stood there like she hadn't even heard. Then she finished slicing and wiped her hands on her apron. She wiped her knife on a towel. She coughed a couple times, cleared her throat. She went up the stairs and talked to Nana.

And then Nana talked to me.

Maybe I listened wrong. Maybe it was because I was young. She sat me down and talked to me and that night I dreamed about him and the next day was when I knew.

That my father was beneath things.

That he was underground.

I walked around the rest of that year. I was in kindergarten and I didn't like to talk. They sent me home with notes about it, but still I didn't change. There were gopher tracks on the schoolyard, all these humped little trails. You could step down where the earth was bubbled and put your foot into their cave. Tunnels. I didn't know it was stupid. What I knew was my father, and I decided he lived down there and he'd made himself small. I'd walk the playground, around by the fence where there was barbed wire, and all the other kids would be on the monkey bars or seesaws, or they'd be playing tetherball, or football, or maybe even tag. But me, I was following the tunnels. I was dropping down and digging with my fingers. I was tracking burrows, pawing the earth, finding not my father, but dark that kept going. And every time I dug, I thought I would find him, and every time I didn't I was maybe a little glad, because that meant I still could find him, and it was like he was always there.

Early autumn sunlight. Leaves edged in amber. Hickson reaches between his knees and levers the mower into first. He makes a pass along the fence at the rear of his property, lowers the deck, and comes by the flower bed on the yard's east side. He cuts another swath, two feet in width, then brakes, shifts into neutral, and steps off the rumbling seat. The air has a crisp scent to it. It smells, to his mind, of clover or cane. Hickson kneels in the grass, making a tripod of his fingers, pressing them into earth. The green blades scratch the webbing between his knuckles and Hickson tests again. Uneven patches. Dips in the ground for which he'll have to adjust. He rests a moment, then places his palms on the ground. He brings his temple within an inch of the lawn and sights carefully toward the house.

Not quite level.

Not entirely plumb.

You can never, it occurs to him, get it right.

He does this daily. Sometimes twice a day. In the springtime or summer when they've had a lot of rain. The clean lines and clear patterns of light green against the darker—it makes him calm,

Hickson. Makes him feel at home. People will say what they say, but Hickson has forgotten people. There's a great deal he's forgotten. He likes to cross his lawn back and forth on the mower. It gives his world angles. A frame.

He climbs back on the mower and shifts into gear. He presses the accelerator, makes a pass, two passes, comes back around to make a third. He is circling the elm shading the north fence when a shadow jerks from the corner of his eye and he cuts the wheel sharply to avoid it. Hickson pulls out of gear, sets the brake, and turns to look behind him.

What he's missed by three inches is not a shadow.

What he's missed by three inches is a hole.

Hickson sits. He kills the ignition and the mower shivers into silence. He starts to get up, but finds he can only sit there, staring. He looks at the hole and he looks at the sky and he stands, straddling the seat, attempting to see over the back fence. He doesn't believe it. He crossed the swatch of grass not twelve hours before. It is plainly there, but it is plainly odd, and Hickson's life has become increasingly even. It has smoothed out into a flat, level plane. He sits there and sits there, but it doesn't go away. Finally, he steps down and approaches the hole, lowering himself, moving more slowly the nearer he comes.

The hole is circular, perfectly round. It is roughly the diameter of a garbage can and, stepping to its edge, Hickson cannot see the bottom. Below him the sun lights ten or twelve feet, the earth dark and newly cut. Beyond that is black. He kneels beside the hole and runs a hand along its rim. The dirt nearer the surface is drier, a layer of dried soil that crumbles beneath his palm. He looks at his house and then behind either shoulder. He stands, walks across the yard, and stares over the fence. His pickup parked in front of the drive. The same street and the same oaks on the other side of the street and a slight breeze on which floats an occasional leaf. He walks back to the hole, kneels, and, lying on his stomach, slides in an arm. Roots and clay and small fragments of rock. He sits back on the balls of his feet and brushes his hands down his jeans. He begins to examine the grass around the hole. He begins to crawl around on his hands.

He thinks, for a moment, he'll go inside and get the tape measure. He thinks about a ball of twine. He thinks about a weight at the end of the twine, and then he just sits. He wonders should he call someone. He wonders who that would be.

Hickson stands, walks across the lawn, and up the steps of his deck. He goes in through the back door, crosses the dining room, retrieves his phone from its cradle on the kitchen wall. He starts to dial an emergency number. He turns the phone on and presses the number 9. He looks at the receiver's digital readout, and then he turns it back to OFF. He dials Parks and gets his answering machine. He dials his cell phone and gets the same. Hickson stands there a moment, tugging the thatch of beard below his bottom lip, and then he seats the phone in its charger and walks back out the door.

He goes down the steps, across the lawn, over to his rear gate. He lifts the latch and lets himself into the adjoining yard. The grass is a foot deep in patches, burned to topsoil in others. There are beer cans and Coke bottles and an aluminum boat that rests upside down on concrete blocks. He steps onto a cracked cement patio, stomps his boots several times, approaches the sliding glass door in back of Parks's house, and knocks. He waits a few moments and knocks again. From down the block, birdcalls. The sound of a phone. Hickson knocks a last time, tries the door, then presses his face to the glass, shielding his eyes with a hand. The blinds pulled halfway, the television on. Pizza boxes on the coffee table and a video game console left out in the center of the room. He calls for Parks once more, and then recrosses the yard, steps onto his property, closes the gate behind him, and fastens back the latch.

Turning, he stands there, watching the hole. He's waiting for it to vanish. Things in his life have done that. People. They are there and then they are not. Hickson takes a knee and sweeps his hand around the rim.

Standing, walking to the mower, he climbs aboard, trips the ignition, and pulls beneath a small lean-to at the rear of his house. He steps off, takes the key, and clips it to the ring of keys on his belt. He covers the mower with a green and yellow tarp on which JOHN DEERE is embroidered in black. He goes back to the hole and casts it a final glance. He toes the grass along its edge and a few loose blades fall over and pinwheel steadily down.

At work, a few hours later, Hickson is placing a fifth call to Parks's answering machine when his walkie-talkie begins to vibrate. He fetches it to his mouth, tucks away his cell, and tells the man on the other end to go ahead.

"You seen J.T.?" the voice asks.

Hickson says he hasn't.

"You seen the greens on Nine?"

Hickson tells him not yet.

"What time was he supposed to water?"

"Six."

"It's burned to absolute shit."

"All of it?"

"Whole shooting match. Thirteen looks like utter hell. Sixteen's going to fry, it gets any hotter."

Hickson stands a moment. On his workbench is a rake handle and a cast aluminum head. A vise and a jar of screws. A tube of epoxy.

"You want me to get him?" Hickson asks.

"Yeah," says Dresser. "Go get him. Bring him up."

Hickson clips the walkie-talkie back onto his belt. This, now, atop everything else. Teenage employees. Immigrant workers and kids. He runs a hand through his beard and then locks the door to the shed and walks over and climbs onto the seat of his cart. He trips the brake and pulls onto the path, the whine of the engine pitching higher as he trundles down the lane. A few singles and groups of three and four. Carson McGinnis in the fairway on Number Five. The druggist stands straddling his ball with a five-iron in one hand and a pitching wedge in the other. He looks like a scarecrow to ward off birds. Hickson gives a brief wave and drives along the path, the grass around him even and bright.

He tops the hill on Seven, crosses the bridge at the shallow end of the lake, and pulls beside a row of birch. He sees where J.T. has parked his cart off-path, just at the edge of the rough. The flag down alongside it. His cup-puncher leaned against the rear of the cart. Hickson shakes his head. How many times has he told him? He sets the brake and walks over to the green to test the grass against his palm. The color has bleached to a light shade of brown, ashen in places, almost white. There is no moisture to it. Squatting, he looks up, and as he does, the boy emerges from a dense stand of oaks. He wears a white T-shirt and blue shorts, the shirt so large its hem falls below his knees. He is thin and short, his skin a light brown, an almost metallic look to it, as if bronzed. He carries a ten-gallon bucket on his hip and he doesn't seem to see Hickson. *Look at me*, thinks Hickson, and then the boy does. He stops midstride and sets the bucket at his feet.

"You're not supposed to go down there," Hickson tells him.

The boy stands blank-faced. He scratches an ear.

"It's private property," says Hickson. "It belongs to the Briers."

The boy stands. He wears unlaced high-tops and his socks are pulled all the way up his shins. Hickson can't imagine how he doesn't trip.

"You water?" Hickson asks.

"Yes."

"What time?"

"I don't know."

"Why's your green burned?"

"I don't know."

"You know what it's going to cost us to fix?"

J.T. looks at him. He looks at the ground.

"You don't care, do you?"

"I care."

"Yeah," says Hickson, "I can see. What were you doing in the woods?"

"Nothing."

"Nothing?"

"No."

Hickson watches him a moment. He passes J.T. most mornings on his way in to work. Stumbling along the side of the highway. Hickson has caught himself wanting to lecture the boy, give him lessons on how to walk.

"Dresser wants you up at the clubhouse," Hickson says.

"Okay."

"He wants you up there now."

"All right."

The boy retrieves his bucket and walks toward his cart. Hickson fits the flag back in the cup and then stands watching as J.T. gathers his things. The boy climbs in the cart and then sets off along the path, inching up the hill by Seven, meandering out of sight. Hickson pulls the back of his wrist along his brow. He walks over and reaches his hand inside the hole and he tries to figure whether this earth would be the same earth as his housing addition across the creek. He rubs several grains between his thumb and forefinger and then stands and looks toward the grove of oaks two hundred yards away. The end of his street. He bought several years back when he was promoted. Any problems, he'd be right across the way. Hickson looks down at his watch. He pulls out his cell phone and dials Parks's number and then stands there, chewing a thumbnail, listening for a voice.

Sundown. Cool and cloudless. Hickson kneels along the rim of the hole, staring into black. The garden hose snakes beside him, and for the past hour he has been feeding in a steady stream of water.

Nothing.

Not even the sound of a splash.

Hickson stands. He turns and walks to the faucet and is twisting the handle when the gate latch trips and then clacks shut. He looks over and sees Parks coming up the lawn. Beer in hand. Jeans and flip-flops and his dog tags hanging between his pectorals. No shirt. His hair still cut in a high and tight.

"What say, Hoss?"

Hickson doesn't answer. He points to the hole.

Cocking his head, Parks walks over and stares.

"What'd you do that for?"

"I didn't do it," Hickson tells him. "It was like that."

"When was it like that?"

"This morning. I went and knocked on your door. I been calling you all day."

Parks gazes intently at the hole, palms on his knees. He sets the beer bottle between his feet.

"That's fucked," he tells Hickson.

"Yes," says Hickson. "It is fucked all the way."

"What did it?"

"I don't know what did it."

"What're you going to do?"

"That's why I been calling."

Parks glances at him. "I was up late," he says.

"I figured."

"Ashley Wheelis."

"Yeah."

"Went to the casino."

"Mm."

"You want to talk about some tits."

Hickson looks over at his friend. He expects the man to be cupping imaginary breasts, but Parks's palms still rest on his knees. He has a lip full of snuff and a sunburn across his face. He's the only man Hickson knows to dip and drink at the same time.

"When," asks Hickson, "you get up?"

"About an hour ago," Parks tells him. He leans over and spits. Hickson watches the tobacco juice drop into the hole.

"How deep is it?"

"I don't know," says Hickson.

"You been filling it with water?"

"I been trying."

The sun has dipped below the horizon. The sky is the color of skin.

"That's Kentucky bluegrass," Hickson tells him.

"You just laid it when?"

"June."

"What'd that cost?"

"About eighteen hundred dollars."

Parks bends down and fingers the grass around the hole.

"It's like it was done with a machine," he says.

"Yeah."

"It's like somebody's cut it with a knife."

Hickson nods.

"Where's the dirt?" Parks asks.

"Isn't any."

"What'd you mean isn't any?"

"I mean," Hickson tells him, "that's how I found it. What you're staring at, that's how it was."

Parks turns to look at him. He looks back at the hole.

"That don't make any sense," he says.

"Tell me about it."

"It's craziness."

"I know."

Both men fall silent. Dusk is gathering, shadows stretching from the trees.

"Maybe it was a well."

"Oil well?" says Hickson.

"Maybe. You know how many they drilled out here?"

"I know there was a bunch."

"Next time you're down at Ken's look at those pictures. There was derricks out here thick as trees."

Hickson kneels beside Parks. "You think it would've fallen in like that?"

"It could."

"Look how it's cut."

"Yeah."

"Look how clean."

"Yeah."

"I don't know a well would do that."

"Might not."

Hickson leans down and puts his head over the hole. He runs his fingers across the dirt inside.

"What are you going to do?" Parks asks.

"Call the city."

"Yeah," says Parks. "And tell them what?"

"That I got a hole in my yard."

"What are they going to do? Send someone out?"

"Have to."

"Why would they have to?"

Hickson shakes his head. "Look at it," he says.

Parks points at the gate to the left side of Hickson's house. The gate, like much of the fence, is new. Parks and Hickson performed the labor themselves.

"How wide's that gate?" Parks asks.

"Three foot."

"So, first thing, gate's coming down."

Hickson looks a moment. His brows furrow. He hadn't thought of that.

"Then," says Parks, "they're going to pull up your roses."

"Yeah."

"And then there's going to be tire ruts from here to the—"

"All right," Hickson says. "I get it." He removes his ball cap and runs a palm across his scalp. Reaching over, he takes Parks's beer and empties it into the hole. He pauses a moment, then drops in the bottle.

Both of them sit there, waiting for the sound.

The next morning, Martin had his secretary upload J.T.'s photograph on the website for Missing and Exploited Children. He had her contact the police department and put out an All Points Bulletin. He sat at his desk drinking coffee, waiting for Lem. He brought up the MEC homepage, scrolled and clicked and stared at the digital image of the boy, his ear-to-ear smile. He thought what Angelica had told him. He thought about the grandmother. Then he minimized the window and sat.

Deputy Lemming came in at nine. He'd had to serve a warrant across town. Six-five, two hundred forty, he'd been a bull rider before taking criminal justice courses at Perser Community. He'd been deputy a little over a decade, and he'd worked under Martin the past four years. Last summer, on a routine pull-over, Lemming found himself in a high-speed chase. When it finally ended, he approached the Toyota the man was driving and ripped the door off the actual frame. Martin didn't know such a thing was possible and part of his job was spent now reining the deputy in.

The sky had clouded that night and it began to rain. It fell several hours, hard, steady, filling gutters along the roads, gathering in bar-ditches and the beds of streams. Martin knew the city park would be flooded, the main entrance where the road dipped beside the town's first derrick. He'd have to send Lem at some point to put up the barricade.

They drove south in Martin's cruiser, crossed the tracks beyond Dawson's Feed, went another half mile, hooked a right, and turned back to the west. During the Oil Boom of the thirties, the town had grown so quickly there wasn't time to build permanent dwellings. On the first floor of the courthouse there were black and white photos of those times, tents and clapboard houses stretching for miles. Blacks and Indians allowed to work in the patch were quartered south of the city proper, and though ninety years had passed, their situation, in Perser, had not greatly improved. Nigger Town, as it was called during Martin's childhood, was a tangle of poorly maintained streets and gravel alleys, dirt paths trailing into pines. Many of the homes were constructed during the Boom—shotgun houses and ramshackle hovels made from cheap lumber and tin.

Martin and Lemming went slowly down the narrow blacktop that served as the central thoroughfare. There were enormous potholes and cracks and Martin could see it'd been years since the county repaved. The rain channeled through the crevices and pooled in the larger holes. You had to go around. With the water standing, you didn't know how deep. Martin flipped the lever to make the wipers go faster. He studied the passing homes. There seemed to be no one about. Windows covered with blankets. Streets deserted. The sheriff's department rarely answered calls from the area. It was rare for a call to be placed. The people here took care of their own living and dying. They had their own markets and cemeteries. Their own stores and grave-makers. They bought and grieved in another dispensation, some other time.

They turned down a side street and then they turned down another. Martin checked his directions and looked over at Lem. The man was sitting there in his uniform, which seemed too small for him, too tight. He looked as if he were surveying an alien landscape. Martin glanced back at the road and saw, through the rain, the mailbox he was looking for up on his left. It was a long white building that sat at the top of a rise between two houses almost identical. There was no car in the drive, but there was a motorcycle, and Martin slowed and pulled in behind it. They sat a moment looking at the overgrown lawn, the house. The swing had come off its hangers and rested on the plankboard porch, two chains dangling above it, slightly swaying. Martin took the keys out of the ignition.

"And what are we here to do?" he asked.

"Talk," said Lem.

"That's right," said Martin. "That's all."

They stepped from the cruiser, walked up the steeply sloping lawn, up the concrete steps. Martin approached the front door, shook the water from his jacket, and knocked. He waited and knocked again. He could hear a television from somewhere inside. What sounded like jazz. He waited another moment and the door opened and a black woman was standing there. She was maybe forty. Her hair was pulled back and done up in rows. She stood there, knuckling the corners of her eyes.

"Help you?" she said.

Martin took off his hat. A runnel of water spilled onto the porch.

"Does a Charles live here?" he asked.

"Yes."

"Charles Whitney?"

"Yes."

"Could we speak with him, please?"

The woman looked from Martin to Lemming, back to Martin again.

"He's down to Dallas. Won't be back till tonight."

"What's he doing in Dallas?"

"Concert," she told him. "Went with his friend."

"Are you his mother?"

"Yes."

"I'm Sheriff Martin. This is Deputy Lemming. Could we maybe ask you a couple questions?"

"What about?"

Martin pulled a copy of the photograph from his pocket and pressed it to the rusted screen door.

The woman nodded.

"J.T.," she said.

Martin snapped the picture back inside his shirt. "He's a friend of your son?"

"He's a good friend," said the woman. "What'd he do?"

"We don't know he did anything," said Martin. "You mind if we come in?"

The woman looked over her shoulder into the house.

"I don't know I'm up to having company," she said.

"You mind coming out to talk to us? Deputy Lemming here is a reformed Catholic. He don't like conversing through screens."

The woman seemed to be thinking about this. She shook her head no.

Martin looked at her. She was small and very thin and she wore a set of hospital scrubs.

"When's the last time you seen him?" Martin asked.

"J.T.?"

"Yes."

"He was over here with Charles, spent the night last Thursday. He has to get up early for his work."

"Your son take him?"

"He walks."

Martin glanced at Lem.

"That's a heck of a walk," Lemming said.

"It is," said the woman. "Four and a half miles. Does it six mornings a week. Charles's buddy picks him up sometimes in the evening."

"Who's Charles's buddy?"

"Ramrod."

"Ramrod?"

"Yeah."

"What's Ramrod's real name?"

"Chris."

"Chris Herring?"

"That's right."

Martin took the pad from his shirt pocket, flipped it open, and wrote, *C. Herring. Ramrod.*

"So," said Martin, "last time you seen him was Friday morning?"

"Last time *I* seen him was Thursday night. Just got in from my shift, he and Charlie were watching TV. J.T. was gone time I got up."

"Has he called here?"

"No."

"You haven't heard anything from him?"

"No," said the woman. "What would I hear?"

"Do you know," asked Martin, "his folks haven't seen him in four days?"

"No," said the woman, and her brow furrowed. "You mean his grandma and them?"

"That's right."

"He didn't go home?"

"No," said Martin. "His aunt was thinking he might have run away."

"Not without Charlie, he didn't."

"Other than him," asked Martin, "anyone else he'd be with? Any other friends?"

"My boy," said the woman, "is the only friend he's got."

On the drive back to Main Street, Martin pulled over for gas. He stood by the pumps, watching traffic. The rain had stopped momentarily. The sky leaked a few drops.

"I don't think she's lying," Lemming told him.

"I don't either," Martin said.

"I don't know she's telling us everything."

Martin asked who did.

"Those boys, though, they're into something."

"Yeah," said Martin, "maybe several somethings. We need them to get back in town. She said they'd be in this evening?"

"This evening," Lemming said.

They stood a moment. A semi passed, trailing the scent of gasoline, exhaust.

"What do we do in the meantime?" asked Lemming.

"In the meantime," said Martin, releasing the trigger on the pump and pulling the nozzle from the filler neck, "we check out his work."

They drove along the red brick streets downtown, turned onto Main. It was red brick as well and in need of repair. There were dips in the thoroughfare. There were bumps. Recently, a petition had gone before the Perser City Council to have the bricks pulled up and asphalt poured, but elders in the community argued against it. The bricks were laid during the Boom, they argued, and they were part of the town's heritage. The petition was denied and to remedy the problem, sections of brick were lifted, the road repaired beneath, then the same bricks placed back over. Martin oversaw the committee that handled the job and he'd been one who supported the elders' claim. He and Lemming went down the wide uneven street, steering around the same dips and divots, which had appeared in the road a few months after the repairs.

They passed the courthouse. They passed the post office and the enormous sandstone building on the other side of the street, the Malcoz Complex. It used to house the sheriff's department and the office of the county clerk. In the morning rain it looked like a castle. They went on down and passed Wisnat's Barbershop and there the brick bled to blacktop and the street forked. They took the road that veered to the right, went across a small bridge, past the soccer field and tennis courts, past the city park and community center. They turned a U in front of the entrance to the Jimmy Hesston Golf Course and pulled into a parking place beside the pro shop. Martin looked over and saw seniors traversing the paved paths on carts, taking advantage of the break in the storm. A bearded man in khaki fatigues and a work shirt came out the front door and walked past the row of vinyl-sided buildings. Cart barns. Toolsheds. Martin and Lemming got out of the cruiser and went up the walk.

Inside the shop, retirees lounged around tables and a vending machine, a television mounted in the corner showing *The Price Is Right*. There were a few clothing racks with golf shirts, displays of clubs and equipment. In the far corner, just right of the counter, stood a short man in his forties with his arms crossed to his chest.

Dark thinning hair. His stomach starting to sag. Martin walked toward him and the man shook his head and released a guffaw.

"Yeah," he said. "It's about fucking time."

Martin had gone to school with the man. His name was Dave Dresser, and he'd been, at one time, Perser's leading light. He'd won numerous tournaments, played through college, and upon graduating he'd made every effort to make it in the PGA. He didn't make it, though. He'd become golf pro at a third-rate course and he drank too much and Martin himself had arrested the man for drunk and disorderly. Martin hoped from the first moment he'd heard J.T. worked at the course that he wouldn't be forced to have dealings with the man, but he stood across from him now, and that hope was gone. He asked Dresser about time for what.

Again, the pro shook his head.

"I put a call in last week. Vandalism on my car. Never heard back shit."

"I didn't get the report," Martin told him. He looked over at Lemming. "Did you get it?"

Lemming stared at Dresser. He told Martin no.

"Do you know who it was did it?" asked Martin.

"I sure as hell do."

Martin stood a moment. He reached in his pocket and pulled out the photograph. "Is this him?"

"It sure as hell is."

Martin nodded. "What'd he do?"

Dresser walked into a small office, rifled through a desk drawer, then walked back and handed Martin a stack of Polaroids. In the pictures, a cream-colored RX-7 had been spray-painted with black squiggles and lines. Dresser had taken pictures from every angle. He'd taken a picture from the driver's seat. He'd even taken a close-up with someone holding a copy of the *Perser Chronicle* in the frame. You could just see the paper's date.

Martin thumbed through the photos.

"You see him do it?" he asked.

"No."

"How you know it was him?"

The man rolled his eyes. "Who else would it be?"

"You fire him?" asked Martin.

"Yeah, I fired him. Our greenskeeper, I thought he'd do a cartwheel."

"When was this?"

"Be a week this Thursday."

Martin took his notepad from his pocket and jotted down the date. He asked if this was the last time he'd seen the boy.

"If I don't ever see him it'll be too soon."

"He's missing," said Martin.

"Missing," Dresser repeated.

"That's right."

"Missing-run-away? Missing-got-high? Help me."

The sheriff looked at the pro and exhaled a long breath. He could hear Lemming's breathing quicken beside him.

Martin cleared his throat. "How do you know he sprayed your car?"

Dresser snatched the Polaroids from Martin's hands, shuffled through a few of them, then showed him a broadside shot of the car. On the driver's door someone had written, *MS-13*.

"You know what that is?" Dresser asked.

"You're serious," said Martin.

"Fuck yeah, I'm serious. I don't know who you been—"

"You think this kid's in a Los Angeles gang?"

"I think *he* thinks it," said Dresser.

"You think he thinks it?" said Martin.

"I do," said Dresser. The man studied the sheriff and his deputy. "You know what?"

"What?" Martin asked.

"I have a golf course to run."

And with that, Dresser walked back into his office and slammed shut the door. Martin and Lemming stood a moment. They looked over and saw that the table of seniors had muted the television and turned in their chairs to watch.

Martin snapped the photo and notepad back into his shirt. He reached for the counter to collect his hat, and then stopped himself, because it was Dresser's shop, and he'd never taken it off.

East of the city the buildings faded to evergreen and oak. The highway scrolled between the hollows, the woods marched on both sides. Fifteen miles would bring you to the city of Wewoka, small borough in the center of Oklahoma once popular for its murders. Barely four thousand citizens claimed residence, and it boasted, at one time, the highest homicide rate in the country. When Martin was coming up as a deputy, radio personality Paul Harvey had referred to Perser's neighbor as *Little Chicago*. The town was now in the clutches of the meth epidemic. Gangs were rampant. Industry gone. Those who had prospects fled long ago. Criminal activity in the sister town bled into Perser and citizens were afraid that in ten years meth labs would have settled into their basements as well. Decent folk would flee farther. To Okemah, maybe. To Shawnee. Martin wondered what he and Deborah would do. He wondered about their boy.

The sheriff thought about it often. What was happening here. The land becoming poorer and its residents more wretched. He'd tried leaving, living other places, but other places weren't home, and he couldn't make them feel like it. Upon graduation, Martin had gone to work for the sheriff's department, and then he'd worked for the U.S. Marshals out of cities in the north. He lived, for a while, in Minneapolis, and then came back to Perser and married his first wife. He was installed as deputy and worked alongside Sheriff Casteel. Things were good for a while. And then they weren't. It was like someone had thrown a switch. Desert Storm started, and Lucy miscarried, and in six months they were separated, and in six more divorced. One of their deputies was shot and in a raid on a crack house another had been killed. It felt to Martin that he was constantly losing, and he tried to determine where he'd gone wrong. He wasn't the same, or the job wasn't the same. He'd look at his town and all he'd see was decline. The more effort exerted, the worse things would get, and he began to fear anger would get the best of him. He began to fear carrying his gun. He had a friend in the Forest Service in southern Colorado and the man offered him a position as fire patrol in the hills. Martin said he'd think about it. Then he resigned his post and moved.

Sitting watch in the tower, looking westward across the valley, Martin would study the sunset and feel himself sinking. That was the stretch of months where he couldn't go back and he couldn't leave and he couldn't sit anymore, thinking. He thought about his brother. About his home in disrepair. People said you couldn't prevent it. Martin told himself he shouldn't have to watch.

He tried to picture his home the way it used to be. He tried to picture what his brother would have been like had he lived. How he would have looked. Martin would stand at the railing and dream. Pete had been a smart boy, good at math. The sheriff decided he would've gone to college, entered the Air Force, ROTC. He would've become a pilot, learned to fly, and when he got out of the service he would have gone to work for the airlines. Martin could see him so clearly, nodding to folk as they stepped aboard his plane. He'd had such heartache over his brother, and these fantasies seemed to soothe it, give him control. They were detailed, very elaborate, and for a long time, they were enough.

But the loneliness got to him, changed him some way, and he said, *If I am to die, let it be at home.*

So he went back. And he had to make a living. He took the job with the sheriff's department. It was really all he knew. He took the job, and one summer during the Gusher Days festival he was manning the corner next to the Lions Club dunk tank, and up came Deborah Stewart and asked where were the restrooms. She was recently back from the Gulf War and her hair was very short. She was twenty-seven years old and she had a round face and high cheekbones and in high heels she stood just five-foot-one. Martin was close to six-two in his stocking feet, and he'd pointed her to the row of blue plastic port-a-johns standing just behind him. Deborah looked at them a moment, then back at Martin. She asked if he was out of his mind.

And that was that. The next spring they were married, and Martin thought to himself, he never talked this way to Deborah, but he thought: *I'll have someone to grow old with and someone with whom to die.* And then Casteel stepped down as sheriff and everyone encouraged Martin to run, and Deb, she thought he certainly should, and so he ran unopposed and he'd been sheriff ever since. In Colorado, in the tower, he went farther and farther away, and then back in Perser it was like his surface constantly expanded. It was he and Deborah. It was the two of them and the town.

And now they'd have a son. He'd grow up one day to have these same struggles, and Martin would teach him the selfsame lesson. What a moment's slip would cost you. The price of letting your vigilance flag.

He took a left off 270 onto a narrow road that would bring them around the back side of the lake. Ash and persimmon trees canopied the road, and Martin began checking the mailboxes. He slowed the cruiser, saw the drive up ahead. He glanced over at Lemming and then he pulled in.

A trailer sat in the middle of ten acres, a single-wide seated on concrete blocks. There was a four-wheeler parked in front, an eighties-model Cadillac with patches torn from the vinyl top. A rickety pine porch led up to the trailer's front door and, sitting on the porch, a middle-aged woman with dirty blond hair done up in braids. She crouched there on the top step with forearms braced against her knees, smoking a cigarette. She had deep lines in her face. A black T-shirt with the name of some band. Blue jeans. Barefoot. She eyed the sheriff and his deputy as they stepped from the car, and exhaled a thin jet of smoke.

Martin walked over and stood in front of her. He took off his hat.

"Mrs. Herring?"

"Yeah."

"I'm Sheriff Martin."

"Okay."

"This is Deputy Lemming."

A grin extended across the woman's face and curled the right side of her mouth. Her cheeks were sunken. When her lips parted Martin could see she was missing teeth.

"What do you want?" she said.

"Your son," said Martin.

"Yeah?"

"Chris."

"Uh-huh."

"We'd like to talk to him."

"Yeah," said the woman, "he ain't here."

"He's in Dallas?"

"Dallas," the woman said. "Went down with his colored friend."

Martin studied her a moment. He removed the picture from his pocket. She glanced at the photo and handed it back.

"Don't know him," she said.

"His name is J.T.," Martin told her. "His folks believe he's gone missing."

"Missing?" she said.

"Yes, ma'am."

The woman reached down beside her and took a pack of cigarettes from a tobacco purse. She selected one and lit it off the cherry glowing between her lips. Then she swapped old cigarette for new and tossed the butt toward the bottom of the steps. It lay smoldering in the grass.

"That all you want?" she asked.

"You expect Chris this evening?"

The woman nodded. "He's got work in the morning," she said.

"Where's he work?" Martin asked.

The woman shook her head and looked off at something in the distance. "Just full of questions, ain't you?"

Martin glanced at Lem.

"Is your husband about?" he asked.

"No," said the woman. "Overseas."

"Iraq."

"That's right."

"He's in the Army?"

"Reserves," she told him. "Unit got called. Go off playing soldier. Leave me sitting here."

Martin stood. He thumbed a card from his billfold and asked would she have her son contact him when he got back.

The woman took the card and stared at it. She shrugged.

Martin thanked her. He and Lemming walked over and climbed inside the cruiser. They sat several moments and then Martin backed down the drive. He turned onto the road and headed for town.

"She was something," said the deputy.

"I'll say she was."

"That hair."

"Yeah."

"And those teeth."

Martin nodded.

Lemming looked over at him. "From the crank, right?"

"The crank," Martin said.

They sat in their recliners, eating supper. Martin had stopped to pick up chicken and he had the TV trays pulled in front of their chairs and the jug of sweet tea on the end table between them. Deborah's was a rocker-recliner, and she would sit with her legs crossed beneath her, spooning mashed potatoes to her mouth and toggling buttons on the remote.

"What do you do about it now?" she asked.

Martin swallowed and shook his head. "We still don't know we're not dealing with a runaway. We can't do much of anything till his friends get back."

"He doesn't sound like a runaway to me."

"Doesn't to me either," Martin said. "Lem said it: 'If he didn't take off with his buddies, he didn't take off.' "

Deborah nodded. She changed the channel. She turned to him and put down the plate.

"You checked the friends, you checked the work. I don't know what else you can do."

"Yeah," said Martin.

"I know you hate waiting."

"Yeah," Martin said.

"You said he walks to work?"

"He walks," said Martin. "He goes and spends the night with his friends, and then walks in in the morning. He only stays home when he's off. The family doesn't own a car. They have a relative takes them in and out of town."

"Where's he go to school?" asked Deborah.

"He doesn't," said Martin. "He quit."

Deb sat there a moment. Then she leaned forward and rolled out of the recliner. She walked by and kissed the bald spot that had appeared atop Martin's head, then stepped into the kitchen. Martin turned and watched her go. He looked over at her hobby table on which sat the completed Phantom. She'd applied the dull coat and was just waiting for it to dry. She'd already started her next fighter. An F-15. There was a plastic frame of miniature parts sitting beside her recliner that she'd begun to clip and sand. Martin reached over and took up a small missile, half the length of his index finger. He sat there studying it, thinking about the boy. If the friends came back with a straight story, he'd have to organize the search, release details to the paper. He'd have to drive back out to the house in the woods and talk with the grandmother, tell her they were looking for her grandson's body. Martin dropped the missile into its box and pinched the space of skin between his eyes. Deborah came back in, sat down, and pulled her hobby tray nearer her chair. She took up what looked to Martin like a section of wing. She folded a swatch of fine-grain sandpaper and began, very carefully, to abrade the nubs of extraneous plastic. Martin sat watching her, the curve of her belly. He thought you could have so much in the world and just like that it could vanish. He didn't understand that. He thought he never would.

He couldn't sleep that night. He just kept tossing. Around three in the morning he stepped quietly from bed and pulled the door to behind him, went down the hallway in his socks. He was thinking of the boy and he was thinking of his brother. He'd lain there, turning his pillow to find the cool, and something about it, the two of them had become tangled in his mind. He was concerned about the boy, but he realized he was more concerned than he should have been, and he lay there wondering how concerned he should be. He thought of the grandmother. Then he rose and left the room.

In the den, he sat at his desk, pilfering through the center drawer. He pulled out a money clip made from a 1922 silver dollar, and then he pulled out the belt buckle that it matched. At the back of the drawer he found it, an old envelope gone yellow with age. He opened the flap and sat there, shuffling photos. Black and whites, mostly. From when they had their house on the river. Martin was just seven when they moved and the property hadn't been occupied in years. This was 1969, outside Cleveland, Oklahoma. That first summer they had scorpions so bad they had to place their bedposts in cans of kerosene so they wouldn't crawl up them in the night. He could remember getting up to use the bathroom, shaking out and slipping on his sneakers, crossing the room to a sound like fortune cookies crunching underfoot.

Martin flipped through the pictures till he came to Pete. On the upper edge of the photograph the drugstore had printed the date: *May 17, 1971.* Pete would have been about six years old. He'd drowned that next year, August of '72. In the picture, he and Martin were seated on rocks at the top of the bluff and between them, old Dempsey, their father's pit bull. They were wearing white T-shirts and tan shorts and one of Pete's shoelaces had come untied. Martin studied the picture. He couldn't remember who had taken it, maybe his father, maybe Uncle Jess. Martin was smiling in the photo, but Pete had a scowl on his face. They'd probably been into it. They wrestled all the time. They did everything all the time, everything together. They shared a room and slept in the same bed.

And then the oddest memory. One winter night. They were both asleep and Martin was dreaming of a fountain or falls and he woke up and Pete had peed all over him. He'd done it in his sleep. Martin belted him in the shoulder and his brother awoke crying. The sound rousted their parents out of bed and they ended up getting switched for it, he and Pete both. They didn't have a washer then; their mother took all the laundry into town. They spent the rest of that night giggling on a pallet. It was funny after the fact.

Sitting there, thinking about it, Martin began to chuckle. He remembered the sound of Pete's laugh so distinctly. He shook his head, cleared his throat a few times, and it was as if something fell down inside him, and the room went blurry, and he had to put the picture away. He put it back in the envelope, put the envelope in the drawer, stood from the chair, and suddenly he was swiping the wet from his eyes, trying to stifle it down. He didn't want to wake Deborah, didn't want her to see this, and he went through the house and outside, crossed the carport in robe and slippers and unlocked the cruiser.

He climbed down inside it, closed the door. He had it, by then, back under control. He sat there, unsure why it got the best of him, feeling frightened and foolish. He shook his head and reached for the door handle, and that was when it really hit him, and it nearly took his breath.

THOMAS SPEAKS

I was older when I heard of Shampe. I was maybe ten. We were at Powwow that summer, at the campground by Maud. It shames me to think it. That I didn't care about Powwow. That I didn't care about nothing but half-pipes and skating. Angelica, she took me anyway. She said these were my people and I needed to go. I'd met Charlie by then and I'd heard at the campgrounds there were sidewalks and a concrete parking lot and I knew we could ride our boards. Whenever we skated, we had to go to town. Out here in the country it's all just gravel, and even where Charlie is, the roads are rough blacktop and there's too many holes. Too many cracks.

What is the word?

Et cetera.

So me and Aunt Angelica, we picked Charlie up and when we got to the campgrounds, there was plenty of concrete and already people skating. Bobby Thomas was there. His cousin Mike. It was July and hot, but we skated the sun down, and when we went over to the picnic tables, there were Indian tacos and Cokes.

It was like a fair. There were booths and bunks and smaller kids flying kites made of string. They looked like nets. People milled and sat on the grass. They spread blankets. One man backed his pickup to the curb and began to unload these ancient drums. He had his hair grown long and twisted into a braid.

The Elders, they told us, were preparing a dance. Had a huge bonfire —like a brush pile ablaze—and as it got darker the flames rose higher and sparks chased the stars. The old men were gathering. Some beating drums. It was like you'd see in the movies if they made movies like that. The younger men had costumes—boots, and turquoise, and the old men had their headdresses. They went around the fire in a circle: left foot, right foot, left foot, right foot. And all the time the Elders were singing in that lost, lonely way which is how you'd feel before a car crash if you were with your family and knew you would die, but you were still, right then, together and alive. I had to look away. They'd go left foot, right foot, left foot, right foot, and one threw back his head and cried at the night. You could feel your heart pulsing in your throat.

There was storytelling. A man named Enoch came and they got a chair for him and a microphone, and a PA was set somewhere in the dark. Mr. Enoch. He didn't look like the other Indians. He didn't sound like them either. His voice had that whispered hush of fire. You didn't want it to stop. He told about Creation. Coyote. Stories on Elk and Bear. He talked it seemed like hours, and someone finally asked for one last story, and he asked what did we want to hear. People mumbled different things and looked at each other. A woman in front of me looked at her lap. A man rose up and said something in Creek. He and Enoch spoke back and forth. Like talk in a prayer. He'd just sat down and a man across from him was standing when a shout came from the darkness, and everyone got completely still.

I turned to ask Charlie what was said.

"Shampe!" called the voice, and folk began to mutter and twitch.

Enoch just sat there. He looked, of a sudden, very old. The lines in his face were like lines cut in wood. His hair was long and silver. It was gathered in a ponytail at the back of his skull. No one said anything. You could hear logs crackling in the fire.

I thought maybe he wouldn't tell it. I thought there'd be something else. A breeze blew streams of cinders.

Then Enoch began talking.

He talked for a very long time.

He was a creature, Enoch told us. Oldest. The deepest dweller. We were all, at one time, of his breed. All of us. The Indian Peoples. Darkness. No memories. We were forgetters, he told us. But we came topside and began to gather. We made homes and huts and traveled. Shampe, though, he kept himself below. Took no bride. Took offspring to him one by one. All his life, said Enoch, was the bottom of things. He made the soil his home.

Enoch looked at his hands. He closed his eyes. He said one last thing I can remember and I can remember it word for word.

"Elders," said Enoch, "would speak of him when I was a boy. Now I am an Elder and no one speaks but me. It is said of Shampe he is a vanisher. It is said of Shampe he makes his way beneath. At all times a miner, he comes topside in greatest night or need. He slips through weeds and windows, carries off the wayward child."

Then he looked up.

"He is not a story," he warned. "He is not a tale to amuse. Shampe is our commitment. We have obligation, each and every one."

That was all. There was no clapping. The moon in the sky was bright and round. People sat for a while. Enoch rose from the chair and walked away.

I stood and started to follow. I didn't know where he was going. I didn't know what to say.

He walked to one of the picnic tables where there were several Indian boys waiting. One handed him a Styrofoam cup and he drank from it. Then he seemed to sense me and turned to look. His eyes were gray and fierce. His mouth a crease.

I stood there, wordless. This man who, not even knowing, had told a story like the story of my birth. I felt myself tugged to him. Drawn like a string tied to me, pulling.

He stared at me a moment.

Then he turned his back.

Charlie fell asleep on the drive home. I was in the backseat beside him, looking out at the night. I thought about Enoch and what he'd told us.

And right then I knew several things at once.

I think the main thing I knew was that my father was gone. He wasn't underground or tunneling. He wasn't coming back. My thinking before this had been wrong thinking.

So I stopped it.

Let it go.

But now a different thought started. It's like when you get rid of something. There's always something takes its place.

Usually it's a bad something.

And what it was this time was that I quit believing in my father. I quit believing he was under things. Quit looking. I started believing in Shampe instead. I don't know how to explain it. Things got swapped. And while before I was trying to get to my father and find him, now I was running from Shampe, who'd be coming to get me.

And I think this was when I realized.

I didn't have much time.

Hickson turns off the television and sits. He glances at the clock in the wooden frame just right of the bookshelf and its various knickknacks. His collection of knives. His grandfather used to collect them and many of the ones on this shelf are from him. Hickson likes how they look. In their cases. Some on little swatches of velvet he purchased mail-order from a store in Tennessee. Hickson stands and walks to the bookcase. Karen used to have his medals out when he first came home, but eventually he made her put them away. She used to have knickknacks of her own. Frogs. Ceramic and stuffed and some of them carved from pieces of soapstone or glass. She took all of them when she left. Hickson picks up one of the knives—German-made Hen and Rooster with a bone handle—and pries it open. He can see a shard of himself reflected in it. Self-portrait in the blade. He polishes the steel against his shirt, closes the knife, and positions it back in its case. He walks over and stands at the sliding glass door.

Outside, it is fully dark. The yard in shadow. Hickson can see, beyond the fence, light from Parks's windows. His back door.

Sometimes he keeps them on till morning. These are better nights for Hickson. He sleeps easier these nights.

He stands a couple more minutes and then slides the door on its groove and steps onto his deck. He reaches inside and flips on the porch light. He can see the hole without it and he flips it back off. He walks back inside and into the kitchen and unplugs his Coleman flashlight from the wall socket and then walks through the house and onto the porch and goes down the steps. The narrow beam of light bounces in front of him. He slows and shines it on the hole. He searches the lawn around it and then he comes onto his knees and aims the flashlight down its throat.

It is cool outside. The grass wet against his jeans. Hickson stares. With the flashlight, he can see twenty feet. Maybe thirty. Beyond that the light disperses. There's just the black. He shifts the beam and examines the walls of the shaft. Perfectly smooth. He lies on his stomach and leans over the hole. There's something down there. He can feel a breath on his face. The air warmer. He stands and walks a few feet and closes his eyes and tries to check. The temperature on his face. He looks to the houses on either side of him. Then he lies back down beside the hole and turns on the flashlight and peers in. The air is warmer down there, he's sure. It feels warm against his forehead and cheeks. It's because the earth is warmer, he thinks. It's warmer than the surface. He wonders is this true. How he knows it. Before going overseas, his Ranger unit was shipped to a base in Minnesota, and there was a man in cadre who showed them how to make shelters in the snow. Using snow. They were leaving in two weeks for desert, and they were in Minnesota making snow shelters. It strikes him he didn't wonder at the time.

Hickson turns off the flashlight and labors onto his feet. He stands there. He won't be able to do anything until morning, but somehow he can't leave. He thinks maybe he should block the hole. Make a barricade. If someone were to come over his fence and fall inside it. Vandals. He's had them before. They might fall inside and then there would be crews of people in his backyard and cranes and media. Hickson tugs at his beard.

He considers the mower, but it's nearly eleven, and he doesn't want to start it. He ends up using rakes. Rakes and shovels and a wheelbarrow and a couple of garbage cans. When he's done, what he's created is a mess, but he thinks it adequate. He pulls at the neck of his T-shirt, and then goes back up the steps. He goes inside the house and locks the door and pulls shut the blinds. He turns off the lights in the living room and then he turns off the lights in the kitchen and then he goes down the hallway and brushes his teeth. He walks back to the bedroom and pulls off his jeans and his shirt. He sits, for several minutes, on the side of the bed. He reaches over, turns off the lamp, lies back on the mattress. Crickets from the bushes just outside the window. Crickets and frogs. He listens for about five minutes. Then he leans up and turns on the lamp and crawls out of bed. He goes back down the hallway and through the living room and over to the door. He pulls back the blinds and stares at his yard. Beyond the fence, Parks's house sits in shadow. Hickson stands there. On the wall beside him are framed pictures of kinfolk and friends. His grandfather aboard a carrier in the South Pacific. His uncle seated in a chopper, 1967, maybe, '69. Another which is black and white of Hickson's father propped shirtless against a bamboo fence, wearing tiger-striped fatigues and sunglasses, holding an M16 slightly slanted and propped against his thigh—two days before he was killed in the raid on Khe Than. Hickson looks back through the glass.

He stands, staring.

He stands there for a very long time.

Midnight now, and Hickson dreams of tunnels. He has come to a place within a place, crossbeams and kerosene lanterns; sandstone; structures of clay. In a widened hallway, corridors branch all directions. Rough-hewn, cracked, a colony here, refuse from topside—road signs and rusted scraps of tin. From down the passage, murmurs, the chink of iron. Hickson's shadow gathers behind him, the floor against his feet like powder or cloth. He rounds a corner and the gleam along the walls begins to brighten. His dream alters and he awakens to birds.

It is Saturday morning. October twenty-eighth. Hickson wakes Parks at ten and they drive to the Lowe's in Shawnee. Parks looks over at him as they make their way down the interstate. His eyes are bloodshot, sleep crusted in their corners. Though sunburned, his skin has a paler cast. He knuckles his eyelids and runs a hand the length of his face. It makes the sound of sandpaper scraping oak.

"Last night," he says.

"Who?" Hickson asks.

"Tami."

"Tammy Jackson?"

"Hell, no," Parks says, "Tami Novotny."

"I thought Tami was married."

"She was married."

"I mean," says Hickson, "I thought she still was."

"You thought right," Parks says.

They drive. Hickson coughs into his hand.

"How're you doing?" Parks asks.

"I'm fucked is how I'm doing."

Parks shakes his head. "Just a hole, Hick."

"Yeah," says Hickson. "How'd you like it in your yard?"

Parks sits a moment, staring out the passenger-side window.

"Good point," he says.

They spend hours walking the aisles, stacking, on a flatbed dolly, sacks of cement, Potter's Earth and Daub. It is Parks's notion that, however deep, there is a bottom to the hole, and to fill it they must seal it at the base. So no water seeps through. No moisture through the pores.

"We seal it," Parks tells him, "and it'll fill."

That afternoon, they mix the powder in ten-gallon buckets and pour it, pound by pound, into the hole. They stand in the October light, waiting.

"How long," asks Hickson, "this supposed to take?"

"Couple hours," says Parks. "Shouldn't be more than three."

"How long does it take concrete to set?"

"Concrete'll take a little longer. Usually give it overnight."

"This is quicker, though?"

"Oh, yeah."

"Why is it quicker?"

"More silicon, I think."

Hickson stares at him. "How many times you done this?"

"This'll be the first."

Hickson shakes his head. He walks to his back porch and then sits there turning the plain platinum band on the ring finger of his left hand.

That evening, they stand over the hole with their garden hoses, feeding it water. The water keeps pouring and it is dark before Hickson closes the valve.

"Drop something in there," Parks tells him.

"Do what?"

"Drop something in."

Hickson retrieves a small stone from his flower bed and pitches it into the hole. They stand an entire minute, waiting for sound. Parks crouches, palms cupped behind his ears.

"Three hundred dollars," says Hickson.

"I'll be damned," Parks says.

Monday morning, Hickson finds J.T. by the sand trap on Three and waves him over to his cart. He points to the boy's rake.

"Grab your stuff," he tells him. "Get in."

Hickson drives him to the trap off Six, and then the one on the other side of the lake. He sits in his cart with his sunglasses, watching the boy as he combs at the sand.

"Straight lines," he calls. "Even it up."

The next day, Hickson is waiting for him in the parking lot. He hands him a shovel and motions to a trench beside the cart barn where workers are installing a sprinkler system. He stands with his arms crossed, leaning against the building, telling the boy to dig faster, deep. Several times he walks over and takes the shovel from the boy's hands and shows him how to brace his weight behind the head of the spade. He hands him a pair of gloves. By noon the boy's shirt is soaked through. It hangs about his knees like a damp towel.

"If you want to," says Hickson, "you can take that off."

The boy stares at him. He shakes his head. Turning to his task, he plants the tongue of the shovel and lifts a spadeful of red earth. His skin glistens with sweat.

Hickson smiles. "Hard work," he tells him. "Probably makes you wish you'd stayed in school."

The boy does not answer him back.

That evening, Hickson is in the clubhouse when J.T.'s friends pull into the parking lot in an '89 Camaro. All of them dressed the same. Baggy shorts and bandannas. Oversized shirts.

"What is it," asks Hickson, "with their clothes? Can they not find anything that fits?"

Dresser stands beside him.

"So they can hide their guns," he says.

Hickson supervises J.T. the next morning. He follows him around on his cart. The boy watering. Changing the cups. Hickson drives to the clubhouse for lunch and, when he comes down the course to check J.T.'s progress, finds him shin-deep in the shallow end of the lake. Hickson watches him several moments. The boy stares into the water, Walkman on his hip and the hem of his shirt bunched up around it, headphones plugged into either ear. He shuffles his feet, then backs up. He retrieves a golf ball. He reaches down and salvages a couple more. Every so often he walks over and drops them in a bucket by the shore. He wades back into the water and continues his search.

Hickson pulls into the lane beside the lake. The boy is walking out of the water with his pockets bulging when Hickson steps from the cart, fetches up the ten-gallon bucket, and holds it out. The boy stands there, staring at Hickson's chest.

"C'mon," says Hickson, jostling the bucket. "Give 'em here."

The boy reaches into his pockets and begins to remove the golf balls one by one. Yellow and white and a bright shade of orange. He pulls out Titleist. Strata and Top-Flite. Wilson Staff. He places them all in the outheld bucket. Hickson asks is that all and the boy pats flat the pockets of his shorts. Hickson grabs the mouth of the bucket with one hand, the bottom with the other, and slings forty or fifty balls back into the water. The boy's neck jerks; his eyes widen. He looks up at Hickson.

"Those aren't yours," Hickson explains. "We got a guy comes in for those every week. He pays us commission. I think that you know."

The boy says nothing.

"How many of those you say that you've took?"

The boy shrugs.

"What're you getting for them? Fifty cents? A quarter?"

"You didn't have to do that," J.T. mumbles.

"Say what?"

"You didn't have to do that."

Hickson studies the boy a moment. He shakes his head, walks over, and climbs into his cart. He puts J.T.'s bucket in the back. The boy mutters something under his breath.

"What'd you say?" asks Hickson.

"Nothing."

"Nothing?"

"Yeah."

A half minute passes, Hickson staring.

"That's fine," he tells him, releasing the brake. "Don't let me catch you saying it again."

Evening finds Hickson squatting over his hole with two hundred feet of kite string and a fist-sized rock. He makes a cradle at one end, cinches it tight, then builds another loop, hitches it over the rock, and makes sure of the balance. He lowers it into the hole and begins feeding out line. He is halfway through the spool when he looks over and sees Parks walking across the lawn. The man comes up, crosses his arms, and nods.

"Cap fell through."

"What?" asks Hickson.

"Cap fell through."

"What cap?"

"Talked to Dad while ago on the phone. He says it's a well. He says what they did—"

"You told Bill?"

"Yeah."

"You mentioned it was me?"

"No, no," says Parks, "I didn't say you. I said 'friend.' I didn't tell him—"

"I just don't want anyone—"

"I know."

"I can't have a bunch of—"

"Believe me," says Parks, "I understand. Dad says they used to cap these things with little slabs of concrete. No telling what was here before they started this addition. Drilling. Land Run. Indians digging tunnels all those years before. Someone comes in, lays down sod, whole time you got these shafts. All that weight's pressing down, you're riding your mower over it, then one day, *pop*—down it goes. Dad said he's seen them break off smooth as a manhole. Happens all the time."

Hickson watches him a moment. He looks back to the string. "So what do we do?"

"Two choices," Parks tells him. "A: we go to the city, in which case this yard's going to look like a coal mine. B: we drive back over to Lowe's, get you a grille or a shed or something."

"Cover it?"

"Yeah."

"We can't fill it in?"

"Not with what you and me can get our hands on."

Hickson doesn't want to cover it. He just wants it gone.

He sits a moment, thinking. He asks Parks, if they leave it, won't it just widen out?

"Dad says no. He says it'll have to fill back up. The hole will fill. Just collapses back on itself. He says way they drill these jobs, the shaft is basically just this—"

"Goddammit!" says Hickson.

"What?"

"Rock slipped off." He shakes his head and begins to wind the string back onto the spool.

"You were wanting to see how deep?"

"Yeah," says Hickson. He sits back on his haunches, wrapping the twine. When he pulls the end from the hole, there is neither cradle nor rock.

"Rock broke your line," says Parks.

"Yeah."

"Must've had a weak spot, something."

Hickson studies the end of the string. Clean break. No ravels or frays. He looks over to the wad of packaging beside him. He straightens the sheet of cardboard on its front. Cartoon of a boy running in grass with a kite hovering behind him. *High-tensile string*, the advert says. *Fifty pound test!*

Hickson stares a moment. It doesn't feel right. There's a stinging in his temples and a cold sensation at the base of his spine. He hopes it's just the way he's sitting, but it's not. He fetches another rock. He ties kite string around it, builds the loops carefully, cinches them tight. Parks watches, nodding with every turn of the twine. When he's finished, Hickson glances up. His friend bent over with hands on his knees. Staring. Intent. They've known each other since elementary. It's the quietest Hickson's seen the man in years.

He rubs a hand through his beard and begins to lower the stone. He dips it into the hole and drops it steadily down, paying out line, paying out more. The minutes string slowly along. Hickson takes his time. A quarter of the spool, half the spool, three-quarters, and then the tension goes suddenly slack. He snaps a glance over to Parks.

"You've got to be shitting me," says the man.

Hickson begins frantically to wind. Parks kneels beside him in the grass, and they both inch closer, and they are in identical postures, genuflecting, when Hickson pulls out the severed end of the string.

The next morning when Martin walked in the front door of the courthouse, Nita stopped him and pointed toward the building's rear wall. At the end of a row of folding chairs sat Charles Whitney, the boy Martin had tried to locate the previous morning. The boy was tall like Martin, bone-thin. He had a shaved head and a long face, narrow wire-rimmed spectacles which lent him a scholarly look. He was hunched over with his elbows on his knees, one foot bouncing. He wore a black hooded sweatshirt, too-large jeans, spotless white sneakers.

"He's been here," said Nita, "since seven o'clock."

Martin took papers from his box and rolled them into a tight baton. He swatted his leg a few times. He told Nita thank you and then walked across the room. The boy watched him come. When he reached the row of chairs, Charles was already standing, and Martin waved the papers and pointed down the hall toward his office. The boy followed. Martin unlocked the door, hit the lights, went over and sat at his desk. When he looked up the boy was standing in the doorway, studying his feet. Martin directed him to one of the chairs.

"How was your trip?" he asked.

The boy came over and sat. He shook his head. He said he was there to help Martin find his friend.

Martin looked at him a moment.

"I was hoping," he told Charles, "he'd be with you."

J.T. wasn't with them. Charles hadn't seen him since Thursday night. J.T. had stayed over, and he'd fallen asleep watching TV. When he woke the next morning, J.T. was already gone.

"This isn't like him," said the boy. "This is bad."

Martin asked if J.T. had ever gone missing.

"Never," said the boy.

"You know anyplace else he'd be?"

"No," said Charles.

Martin sat a moment. He leaned forward and took his hat off and placed it on the desk beside him. He smoothed his fingers through his hair and cleared his throat. He looked Charles squarely in the eye.

"I'm getting ready," he said, "to inconvenience a whole lot of people. Based on what you're telling me. If you're full of shit, I need to know it right now."

"I'm not full of shit," said the boy.

"I mean even a little."

"Yessir."

"The least little bit."

"I understand."

Martin raised a hand and made an inch worth of space between his thumb and forefinger.

The boy looked for a moment. Then he shook his head.

"Tell me," said Martin, "about Dave Dresser."

"We tagged his car."

"Why you'd do that?"

"He's a dick."

"What else you do?"

"Tagged some other cars. Tagged J.T.'s boss."

"What else?" Martin asked.

"We let air out of his tires."

"What else?"

"We egged it."

"All this for Dresser?"

"Dresser," said the boy. "J.T.'s boss."

Martin sat there.

"What else?" he said.

"Nothing else."

"That's it?"

"Yeah."

"No drugs?"

The boy shook his head.

"You sure?"

"Yessir."

"You pass a piss test?"

"Bring it on," Charles said.

Martin ran a palm across his chin.

"Why'd you tag Dresser? Decide you'd pitch a little get-back?"

"Yessir."

"How that work out?"

"I don't guess it did."

"You in a gang?"

"Nosir."

"Dresser said you were in a gang."

"Dresser's a dick."

"I know he's a dick," said Martin. "I went to school with him. Tell me about *MS-13*."

"I saw it on CNN."

"Saw it on CNN."

"Yessir."

They sat there. Martin let the room go very quiet.

"Why'd you come down here to tell me this?" he asked.

The boy had been looking between his feet, but now he raised his head. "I told you. J.T. don't do this. Something's wrong."

Martin studied Charles, and then he looked at his desk. He saw himself walking up those carpeted steps, standing outside the old woman's room. Her daughter between them, trying to translate.

The sheriff stood.

He fetched his hat off the desk and squared it on his head.

"Come on," he told the boy. "Let's go find your friend."

They started by driving the route J.T. took back and forth from work. Charles sat in the passenger seat, leaning forward, showing Martin where his friend would walk. They stopped several times, pulled to the side of the road, and got out. They checked ditches and storm drains. They checked behind sumac bushes and narrow stands of oak. Charles showed Martin where J.T. liked to cut across the tracks. It was just a red dirt path going through the pines. Charles stood there pointing at buildings on the other side of the rails: a lumberyard, the old depot which had been converted into a Mexican restaurant. Martin looked back behind him into the trees. He made a few notes in his ledger and then they went on.

They drove down Malt Phillip. They drove down Walnut and First. Martin slowed the car, turned down a lane, and they went half a mile along an alley that backed several businesses, the funeral parlor, the donut shop. They pulled onto Strothers, drove down to the 9 intersection, then along the highway in back of the course. He turned into the rear entrance, drove the loop, and Charles showed him where J.T. used to hop the fence beside the creek. There was a line of woods extending toward a hill where a housing addition had been constructed several years back. You could just make out a few of the antennas, the tops of trees. They sat there with the car idling.

"And this is always the way he comes?" asked Martin.

"Yessir," said Charles.

"He never comes any different?"

"Not that I know of," Charles said. "He likes the same things. He has a ham sandwich every day for lunch. Mom tries to pack him turkey, but he always wants ham. Mustard. No lettuce."

Martin looked at Charles. He looked over the course.

They drove the rest of the morning, and Martin made maps, drew sketches, a grid. When Lemming got in, he had him run a report out to the grandmother, and he had Nita place a call to the state police. He gave her information for the papers and asked would she make a call to the tribe.

The next day he and Lem, three deputies, and several men from the Chickasaw Tribal Council walked the woods surrounding J.T.'s home.

They searched a persimmon grove, traversed pastures and fields. They walked the length of Cedar Creek and then backtracked, came by the highway, walked it from the opposite bank. They retraced their steps, went back and forth through the woods.

They found nothing.

The boy was gone.

Late afternoon, untangling himself from a patch of briars, Martin ascended a hillside grown with moss and looked down at the slender stream beneath. An old man was sitting on a rock below him watching where the water dropped a foot or so and curved into a sandstone bend. The man was tapping the ground between his feet with a dry hickory limb, and Martin climbed down and stood beside him. His name was Enoch Malcoz, and he wore a cowboy hat fashioned from straw. Blue jeans. A blue western shirt. His silver hair braided and drooped between his shoulders, the end tied with a dark color of twine. The man's ginger skin creased sharply at the mouth, sagged below the chin, but his eyes were fiercely alert and he seemed never to blink. He had young hands. Young shoulders. The sheriff adjusted his gunbelt and crossed his arms to his chest. The old man didn't look up.

"What say, Enoch?"

"Sheriff," said the man.

Martin glanced idly about. One of his deputies and two of the Chickasaw teens working for Enoch were examining a hole in the creek bank about forty yards down.

"You decide you'd come out and help us?"

The old man nodded. He knocked the tips of his cowboy boots with the length of hickory. "Should've worn my shoes."

Martin hiked his trousers and sat. He would see Enoch most days in town. The man was a writer of some repute, an expert on Native American folklore and myth. His books were shelved in libraries across the country. Not that he needed the money. He'd inherited mineral rights from his family. A drilling company. Disposal wells and gas. The Malcozes had settled Perser before the Land Run. They were the city's first tenants. They'd dug the first cellars and laid the first bricks. A story had it that they'd descended from conquistadores, from a Dominican priest who'd gone native in the New World, abandoned his religion, taken an Indian bride. Enoch acted as mediator between tribal and civic authorities, and Martin had often gone to him to help settle matters that sheriffs and courts could not.

"How is Deborah?" Enoch asked.

"Good," Martin told him. "Real good."

"When's she due?"

"Late February, they're saying. Early March."

"Girl or boy?"

"Boy," said Martin.

The old man coughed. He turned to brush at something on his shirt.

They sat a few moments. Martin asked what he thought of all this.

"Feels bad," Enoch said.

"Yeah," said Martin. "Does to me too."

He looked up at the canopy above them, the leaves turned and some fallen, still thick enough to block the sky. You could just see these fragments of blue.

"Did you know the boy?"

"I knew him," Enoch said.

Martin nodded. He thought the man would say more, but he didn't.

The deputies had moved around a bend in the creek. It was just him and Enoch.

Martin cleared his throat.

"We first got the call, I kept thinking he was a runaway. He doesn't turn up in the next couple days things are going to get ugly."

Enoch prodded with the stick. He said things were ugly now.

Martin looked at him a moment. "Let me ask you something."

"Ask," Enoch said.

As Martin opened his mouth to form the words, the crack of a gunshot came from down the creek. He and Enoch stared at one another and then they stood and began walking. They topped the rise and went down through the blackjacks, past large shapes of sandstone that stood out from the blanket of fallen leaves like ancient creatures curled into themselves, frozen. Below them stood two of his deputies and two of Enoch's hands. There was a thin hump of fur at their feet that Martin recognized as a dog and then as a coyote. Lemming and Bunker hovered over it,

Bunker with his pistol drawn, and the Chickasaw teens—just boys, really—stood back a few feet, grim expressions, tightened mouths. When he saw Martin coming, Lemming began to shake his head.

"Annie Oakley," he said, jerking a thumb toward Bunker. "Shoot his way to stardom."

The sheriff walked up to the coyote, started to lower himself, then stepped back when he saw her side rise and fall, heaving. There was a dark red circle beneath her right shoulder and a trickle of red pooling onto the dirt.

"What the hell?" Martin said.

Bunker pointed. He was a squat man with red hair and pimples. He was twenty-five and his stomach overhung his trousers by several inches.

"Sheriff," he said, "it come at me."

"Come at you," Lemming mocked. "Didn't *come* at you. You surprised her, and she took off running."

Martin was watching the animal. Her ears were pinned back against the skull and you could tell she was trying to move her head, but couldn't. She kept baring her teeth.

The sheriff gestured at the Glock forty-caliber in Bunker's right hand. "Why don't you put that away," he said.

The deputy looked at the pistol as if surprised. He holstered the weapon and then snapped the strip of patent leather across it.

Lemming stared at the man. He leaned over and spat. He glanced at Martin, raised his eyebrows, and Martin studied the animal a few seconds and nodded. The deputy unholstered his sidearm and the boys turned away. Martin also turned, placed his fingers to his ears. Enoch had his fingers in his ears also but he was still watching. The gunshot came. The report echoed back through the hills. Enoch pointed to her stomach.

"She's got pups somewhere," he said.

The sheriff glanced back over. Six swollen nodes of pink, fur moistened around them in circles.

"Shit," Martin said.

Bunker began to glance nervously about him.

"What?" he asked. "We got to look for the kids?"

Lemming shook his head. The Chickasaws stared.

"That's right," Martin told him. "You can start by going fetching a shovel."

"Where am I going to get a shovel?" asked Bunker.

Enoch told them he had one in the bed of his truck.

The deputy looked at the ground a few moments. Then he crossed the stream and went up the hill, crunching through the leaves.

They watched him go.

"Fucking dumbass," Lemming said.

They spent the next half hour searching for the den. Enoch said it would not be far. He said it would be a burrow, a narrow place under rocks.

He was right. On the far slope coming off the creek bank they found a worn area beneath a sandstone shelf, a groove rubbed into the earth below the rock. The stones there were large and weathered and lodged against each other, broken. Martin thought they might be able to move them, but they were too big. Bunker came back about an hour after he'd left, walking toward them with the shovel, and Martin took it from him and then sent him for their supper. The deputy knew enough not to complain. Coyotes were sacred to the tribe. You couldn't grow up in Oklahoma and not know it. The trickster, escape artist, Indian folklore was full of his tales. Chickasaws had elaborate rituals for dealing with their burial. They would avoid places the coyote had died. They'd been known to move their homes.

The old man knelt at the den's entrance. He'd borrowed Martin's flashlight and was gazing under the rock. He kept sweeping the beam back and forth until he saw the reflection of eyes.

"Are they in there?" Martin asked.

Enoch bent farther.

"They're in here," he said.

They tried digging out the entrance. They tried loosening one of the stones and going in toward the back. Finally, Enoch had Lem tunnel in the side, move one of the smaller stones, then pry another up. He reached down and began to hand the pups out one by one. Their mother had been gunmetal-gray, but her pups were darker, brown and black. Their heads were belled, the ears small triangles of fur, the snouts yet to elongate, with that almost flattened look. Thick hair. Eyes still closed. Their stomachs swollen with fat. Enoch stood at Lem's elbow with the flashlight. He kept up a kind of monologue as he fetched the animals out.

Coyotes, he said, they went to ground early. They were alert, nervous creatures. Hunted at night. Rabbits and rodents, fish and birds. He'd known coyotes to eat leather. Their young.

They could be taken and made into pets. Enoch had known it to work. The thing about them, some you could raise just like a dog. Some would be inevitably wild. Others occupied a liminal space. They would be gentle for a while, docile while they grew. Then they would turn suddenly and revert. Like deep down they were a wild thing and were only biding their time.

The sun had just dipped below the horizon. Daylight was failing. They sat around the den, each with a pup in his lap, the two boys, and Lem, and Martin, Enoch leaning against the rock and holding a pup to his chest, stroking a thumb along its spine. As if this were no longer a search, but a lecture or outing. Enoch continued speaking. Martin looked up at the man from where he sat against a tree cradling the pup between his knees, listening, the woods going dark. It was like he'd been granted a reprieve from looking and it occurred to him the case had been a sentence, or he'd borne it that way, heavy, hard. It was a sentence because he wanted so badly to find the boy and he seemed to know he absolutely would not. That knowledge and the desire battered against one other and built. With each day of nothing—no details, no leads—the responsibility grew. The guilt.

Martin sat there, stroking the pup. It was full dark now and they'd have to find their way back by flashlight. Birds called from the tree limbs. Sleek-feathered crows. They would squawk to one another in their lost lonely cries, and then carry their black bodies off into night. You would not see them at this hour, only hear from above you the flapping of wings.

He left the courthouse the next evening and drove east on 270. The autumn sun had yet to go down and the air outside was crisp and cool, the sky shifting toward a darker shade. A strange cast, thought Martin. The color of veins. He went past the city limits and then past the brick plant. Trees thickened and in the hollows beside the road a mist rose and curled about the oak branches and pines. He began to meet cars with their headlamps shining and in his rearview the clouds blushed crimson.

Martin drove. He thought about the boy. He'd woken that morning and it was as if something had settled onto his breastbone and begun pressing down. He kept trying to swallow it, but it couldn't be swallowed. The sheriff crossed the bridge by Tanner Creek, tires clicking over seams in the pavement. Up ahead, 270 turned toward Holdenville, but Martin kept to his left. Another five miles and he entered the town of Wewoka.

At the edge of the city, on the hill before you descended, there used to be a sign. *Ryan's Pig Stand. Old fashioned barbeque.* The sign was now missing and the windows were boarded and all along the west side of the building were gang signs and graffiti and etchings in the cinderblock. Caricatures. Cartoons. A rat spitted on the fangs of a rattlesnake. Martin watched the fresco smear by. He slowed his vehicle and pulled into the right-hand lane.

He took a left on Mekusukey and then another onto Park. He turned onto Ocheese and went down the street, studying homes. Many boarded up. Others with bars over the windows. Some with lawns choked by garbage, by weeds. He passed one house where a child sat in the fork of an elm. The tree was near limbless and the boy was perched six feet off the ground with his knees braced against the peeling bark. Martin waved to the boy but the boy didn't wave back. He just sat there, staring.

He drove the streets for the next half hour. Okfuskee and Jackson. Sasakawa Avenue. Mekusukey was the central thoroughfare and like Perser's it had been built from brick. This street, however, had seen little maintenance, and sections of it were roped off and blockaded with barrels. It was full dark now and Martin went slowly. Streetlamps glared atop their poles, many of them shot out or shattered. Up there, the building that used to house the theater. Next to it, what had been a pharmacy. The establishment had a full-sized fountain and twelve leather-covered stools. The counter was a one-inch marble slab. He stared at the building, the windows painted over, one of them bricked up and boarded. Convenience stores and supercenters had sent all of it under. Little left to the town. A few bars and pawnshops and a local drive-in at which there were shootings. The sheriff had wanted to see what Perser could come to. As if it might purge him. He hooked a U and went back down the street.

Back on the highway, Martin thought about the boy. He thought about his brother. Ten years of age, on the banks of the Arkansas, Martin had led Pete into the shallows hunting bait. They had turkey necks tied to pieces of butcher twine and Martin had a gunny sack hitched at his waist. Pete had just turned seven the previous week and he'd begged Martin to take him along. Early that morning they walked to the river and followed it back into the hills.

They were about ten feet apart and Pete kept trailing. Martin would have to watch to make sure he kept up, that he didn't walk into deeper water, that he didn't get caught by driftwood, debris. He'd just glanced back, was going to tell him to come closer, and the boy took a step toward him, and then turned and looked upstream. Water dripped from a tuft of hair that lay lank across his forehead. Crows called in the distance. Pete twisted his neck and stared at Martin. He smiled, edged forward, and then vanished as if through a trapdoor.

Martin had reached for him, but he was no longer there. Circles rippled from the place where his brother had stood. Overhead, the limbs of a willow arched out and dipped.

Sunlight.

A slight breeze.

Other than this there was nothing.

Later, their pastor would explain:

Holes in the riverbank, covered with silt. Just their mouths covered, and beneath them pockets of air. The river swells and in the shallows, sometimes, you will have these spaces, weak patches along the floor. Step onto them and the bottom gives way. You tunnel down, the earth filling in above you, water filling. You are pressed tight and suffocated. In this way you are drowned. They will have no means to find your body. There is no way to look. Sediment clouds the surface and then is swept away. A series of bubbles. A few fragments of loam. In several moments, the river clears.

Martin didn't know this. He'd never heard of silt traps or sediment. He'd splashed back and forth through the shallows, screaming. He dove down again and again and when he came to himself, spots swam before his eyes. There was no body to bury and the casket at the funeral was just for show. His brother was down in the earth somewhere, hidden beneath the river. Martin's mother and father would look at him sometimes and Martin could barely look back. They said it wasn't his fault. An accident, they said. Beyond his control.

He made his decision very young, what he would believe of the world, and what Martin didn't believe were *accidents*. He didn't believe the way his parents would have him believe. They said he wasn't guilty, but Martin, he decided different. He didn't know enough, he decided. If you knew what was waiting, you could equip yourself to face it. If you knew the effects, you could trace them to their cause. What you didn't know, what slipped by you, this would only drag you under. Worse: it would sink the people under your care.

He went into law enforcement for just this reason. His principle was that nothing occurred without motive; nothing occurred without giving sign. He'd seen it time and again. Working in the Marshals Service. Working under Casteel as deputy and undersheriff. Each event trailed evidence like the arrowed ripples that accompany fishing lures across a pond. Track the wave and you discover the thing itself.

On the Arkansas that morning, there were no traces, and Martin had made his way frantically through the shallows, grasping into the water at likely images, reflections broken in the current. There was a space of time he couldn't remember, and then he found himself sitting on the riverbank with knees pulled to his chest. Sitting in the sunlight and shivering, staring while water ran and birds called and cicadas buzzed from the bushes. Everything outside him moving as before, everything inside frozen, gone entirely wrong.

THOMAS SPEAKS

So I went to see Him. I couldn't stop my thinking. I'd go to sleep and dream Shampe. I'd wake and there He'd be. It might've been a story to some people, but it wasn't one to me. He was under the bushes at my middle school. In the storm drains and cellars. He lumbered in the dark patches of the evenings, slipped from the shadows of oaks.

One afternoon, I ducked in an alley on the way home from school. I was in eighth grade by then and I had to take the buses. Angelica would get me up around five and make my breakfast. She'd clean and dress me, pack a second meal for my walk. An apple. Some kind of fruit. I'd walk a mile down the dirt road and then another on the blacktop till I got to 99. I know Nana worried about it, but there wasn't another thing to do. From there I went another two miles along the shoulder of the highway, and then the bus from Harther, a little country school that only went to seventh grade, would take me to the airport on the hill. That was the city limits. A Perser Public School bus would pick me up, take me on in to town. If the driver topped the hill and I wasn't standing there, I'd have to walk another mile.

That afternoon, though, I decided to skip the buses. I decided to go

ahead and walk. I went up Orchard Street, down the hill by the super-
market, along Malt Phillip until I hit the park. I cut across by the derrick,
went down another alley, then on down Main Street toward the square.
It was Enoch's place I was going to and I could already see the tops of his
building.

It's a big one, Enoch's. Wide and tall. The sandstones old and faded,
some red, all of them cobbled together like a street.

I went up and went past it, crossed to the post office, and sat my bag
on the steps. Then I sat. I sat there and stared.

Pigeons were perched on stones above the arches.

Glass in the windows reflected cars.

I went back the next day, but I didn't go in. I went back the next and
the next.

Fall went on by. Winter went by. The spring came and the dreams of
Shampe wouldn't stop. Thinking wouldn't stop. I'd never gotten a grade
in school lower than an A. I was on the Superintendent's Honor Roll and I
was in the Merit Club. I was in Math Club, Science Club, History Club.

I knew that this was ready to change.

And this is how:

I'm the kind of guy, I could get all A's.

I'm the kind of guy, I could get all F's.

I could get all one thing.

Or I could get all of the other.

What I couldn't do was mix.

So the grades slipped. I slipped. Everything started falling. Because of
Mr. Enoch.

Shampe.

It was May and school was almost out and instead of going to the bus
that morning, I cut across the fields. The sun was coming over the trees
and I remember the grass still had slivers of ice. It was cold for that late in
the year. My breath like fog. I went along the east end of the golf course,

down the street, over onto Main. I walked up to Enoch's building. It looked different in the morning pink. There was a glass door on the north end and I opened it and stepped inside.

It smelled old. Everything molded. There was a steep staircase that went up and up. A threadbare carpet. Wood-paneled walls. I climbed the steps and came onto a landing.

To my right was a hall with doors on both sides.

To my left, a man standing.

Mr. Enoch.

He said, "Follow me."

I didn't answer. I stepped right in behind him and we went down the hallway, up another flight of stairs, past several doors, and into a room with tall windows and rocking chairs and a half-finished painting on one of those stands. I don't remember what it was a painting of. I didn't ask. He pointed to a rocker and down I sat and my heels just touched the boards. I scooted forward in the chair. I scooted back and put my feet on the rungs. I couldn't get comfortable. Enoch sat in the rocker beside me and looked out the window. You could see the post office down below.

"Thomas," he said.

I didn't know what to say back. I didn't know he knew me, or how he knew to call me Thomas.

He did, though.

I just sat.

He leaned over and took an apple from the windowsill. He pulled a knife from his pocket and began to slice it into quarters. He didn't remove the seeds like Nana. He didn't even remove the stem. He made four quick cuts, wiped the blade along his pants leg. He handed across a slice.

I took it and nibbled the edge and we sat a few moments, chewing.

Then he asked me what did I want.

I looked at him. I opened my mouth to talk. I didn't really know how to say it. I didn't know where to start.

And so the first thing I told him was that my father was dead and the next thing I told him was that I wanted Shampe. To know about Shampe. More, at least, than what I knew. I said I'd heard him talk at Powwow and he'd spoken of Shampe and that this was why I was here.

He turned to look at me.

His eyes were gray.

His mouth a thin slit.

"Why do you want this?" he asked.

I sat there, trying to think.

I asked how he knew my name.

He smiled. The only time I've seen him do it.

He put a slice of apple in his mouth. He brushed his palm along his thigh and stood and walked across the room. He took a leather book down from a shelf and then he came back over. He sat and began thumbing through.

Then he said—a question, almost: "You are Chickasaw?"

I told him my father was Chickasaw. I told him my mother had been Spanish. Or she spoke Spanish, rather. That she was Mexican. I said that I was half of both.

This time it wasn't a question.

"You are Chickasaw," he said.

I sat there. I felt my hands begin to sweat. I felt like I was floating. As though it wasn't even me.

He said he'd known my father. My father and his father before.

And then he said I was a special kind. Or I'd had special things create me. He used an Indian word I can't remember. Very old word. Very odd. He translated it for me, said it was no surprise I'd be drawn to Shampe, for finally, I was one of him.

I stared out the window.

"What's that mean?" I asked.

"It means," said Enoch, "it is not the fault of your father or mother. It is not the fault of your grandmother or aunt."

"Why?" I asked him, my voice going thin.

"It is a calling," Enoch said.

I sat there and thought about that. My panic was growing.

A few minutes passed.

I put the apple in my mouth.

Finally, I turned to him. I asked if he could make it go away.

"The calling?" he asked me.

I told him the pain.

He nodded. "This suffering of yours?"

"Yes."

"This hurt?"

"That's right."

"You feel as though there is no place for you. As though you will never find a home."

I am ashamed to say it, but then I started weeping. I wept out of fear and panic, because I'd known there wasn't a home for me, and now here was Enoch, and he said the same thing. Or his words said it. I'd wanted this man to show his secrets and all that came out were my own.

An Underchild.

This awful calling.

I could feel my heart running faster and that buzzing in my temples.

He was right. There was no way out of it. No over, across, or through.

There was always this thing inside me.

And now I knew its nature.

I even knew its name.

"What do I do?" I asked him.

"Go under," Enoch said.

The next morning Hickson wakes to find his pickup egged and the tires let out. It is a few minutes after six and the sky in the east is a pale shade of rose. Hickson circles the vehicle in his bare feet and sweatpants, pausing to scratch his thumbnail against dried splotches of white. He walks in the house, changes into his boots and jeans. He starts the coffee and goes to the bathroom. On the vanity, next to his toothbrush and razor, a small plastic container with seven compartments, the days of the week lettered across. Hickson opens THURSDAY, fishes out two salmon-colored capsules, and downs them with a palmful of water. He stands there staring at himself in the mirror. His blond hair thinning in its crew cut. His beard growing darker. Dark circles beneath his eyes. He turns and strikes the wall with the heel of his hand. He strikes it five times in quick succession. A picture rattles crooked in one corner. A light winks out above the sink. Hickson presses his hands together and brings his fingers to his nose. The thing that rises up and feels as though it will split the skin. Then fading. The fall-off and sink. He wipes the wet from his eyes and goes back into the kitchen.

Outside, he wheels the compressor from the garage and fills the tires. He checks the pressure and then fingers the tread for cuts. He goes back through the front door, fills his thermos, drives to the car wash. It takes thirty minutes and five dollars to spray the egg off, but off it comes without taking paint. He spends another dollar on a wax cycle and then goes in to work. Seven-thirty by the dashboard clock. Hickson walks up to the clubhouse, starts the coffee, then sits at a table by the window watching the day compose itself, trying to force himself to breathe.

Fog is evaporating from the hollows.

Sunlight filtering through the limbs.

Evening, he and Parks drive to Lowe's and wander the aisles. It is a large store with massive ironwork shelves, a warehouse with aproned employees and concrete aisles. Smell in the air of sawn lumber. Paint thinner. Steel. Hickson tells Parks about the egging and Parks looks at him a moment and shakes his head.

"Reptiles," says the man.

"Yeah," Hickson says. "I got to empty the garage and see if I can fit in my truck."

Parks runs a hand over his stubbled chin and reaches to slap Hickson on the shoulder. Hickson rebounds a couple steps.

"Brother," says Parks, "you are having a time of it."

"I am."

"Way they treat heroes these days."

"I guess."

They shuffle by a few aluminum structures, checking prices. An employee passes them wearing a back brace and matching suspenders.

"Speaking of," says Parks, "you going next week?"

"I'm not going."

"Come go with me."

"I'm not going down there."

"Only take a couple of hours. Dallas."

"Dallas," repeats Hickson. "I didn't like those people when I was marching alongside them."

At the end of the row is a smaller shed, dark gray in color, a wide door and tented roof. The building kit is on sale for eleven hundred dollars.

Hickson looks over at Parks. "You going?" he asks.

"I'm planning on it. I talked to Captain Morley. You believe that? *Captain?*"

"Been at it long enough," says Hickson.

"What is it now, ten years? Eleven?"

"Well, you count it from '90, '91, '92, '93—sixteen," he tells Parks. "No. Seventeen. It'll be seventeen, December."

"Seem that long to you?" Parks asks.

Hickson lifts the price tag dangling from the handle of a shed door and examines the writing on its back. He says it seems to him like yesterday afternoon.

They purchase the gray shed and a broad-backed teenager loads the boxes into the bed of Hickson's truck. They turn onto the interstate and Hickson accelerates to a mile under the speed limit and then sets the cruise. I-40. Semis passing in the left-hand lane. Bull-haulers. Cattle trucks and the occasional tanker. At the exit to Earlsboro, gas is three dollars a gallon. Hickson points to the sign and asks Parks does he see.

"I see it," Parks says.

"How much higher you reckon it'll go?"

"I hope five dollars before it's over."

"Yeah," says Hickson. "I hope it does too."

He stares down the highway. Off to the side. New production. Lights, in the distance, of new drilling sites. Derricks surrounded by blackjack and pine. Hickson thinks theirs might be the last state that benefits. The rest of the world needs oil to feed it. Oklahoma continues to pull it from the ground.

Parks turns and looks through the slider window at the bed of the pickup. He offers to assemble the shed while Hickson's at work.

"You don't have to do that."

"No," Parks tells him. "Give me something to do."

"You sure?"

"Yeah," says Parks. "Unemployment's about to kill me. Wait too long, mess around, have to go back to work."

Hickson shakes his head. "I appreciate it," he says.

"Course."

"We'll get settled tonight, I'll show you where I was thinking."

"Over the hole, right?"

"That's the idea," Hickson says.

The following afternoon, Hickson is raking the sand trap on Sixteen when his walkie-talkie begins to shudder. He stares, a moment, at his hip, then picks it up and answers.

"Come up here," Dresser tells him.

"What is it?"

"Come the fuck up."

Hickson massages the space between his eyes and then clips the walkie-talkie back on his belt. He climbs in his cart and starts up the path. All day long it has been raining, the sky gray and pillowed with cloud. He turns up the trail by Three, makes his way across the bridge, then pulls into the lane and heads for the clubhouse. He sets the brake and puts the key in his pocket. He takes several steps, and then goes back to the cart and moves where he can see it from the window.

Dresser has a five-iron yoked across his shoulders when he walks inside.

"You'll never believe what the fucker did now."

"What fucker?" asks Hickson. "What'd he do?"

Dresser points to the window. He motions for him to follow.

Outside, Dresser's car is parked at the curb. New RX-7. A dark shade of cream. Tinted windows and chrome wheels and a personalized tag. From the front fender to the taillight someone has spray-painted crooked black lines. Curlicues and circles. The number 13.

"He's history," Dresser tells him. "Done."

Hickson studies the car a moment. He shakes his head.

"I had my truck egged night before last," he tells the pro. "Some kids in the neighborhood—"

"Fuck kids," says Dresser. "You see *that*? This is gang."

"What gang?"

"MS-13," Dresser says. "CNN had a story on it. Mexican. Bad as it gets."

"You think a gang would—"

"You know anything about this kind of shit?"

"No."

"This is how they are," Dresser tells him. "This is what they do. They're the ones down here selling meth to first-graders."

"How do you know all this, David?"

"I told you," screams the man, "I saw all about it!"

Hickson runs a hand through his beard and brings his fist to his mouth. He watches Dresser kneel in front of his vehicle and inspect the paint.

"When's he on schedule again?"

"Monday morning. Monday afternoon."

"You going to wait and talk to him?"

"Fuck, no," says Dresser. "I'm calling the cops. I got to be in Tucson Sunday night."

"I hate someone did that," Hickson says.

"Yeah."

"You want me to see if I can try and get it off?"

"Leave it," says Dresser, "I'll need pictures for the insurance."

Hickson nods. He stands there watching as Dresser squats at the front fender, licks a thumb, and begins to rub it across the paint. His reflection on the vehicle is an inverted smear.

Hickson tears a sheet of paper from his tablet, writes the word *well*.

He sits a few moments, writes the word *hole*.

He writes *shaft*

mine

water

coal

He crosses out *coal*. He scribbles over *mine*. He begins drawing a picture, a diagram of sorts. He draws ground, in it a cavity, all sketched in profile, viewed from the side. A—what do they call it—*silhouette*. He draws for ten minutes and then he puts down the pen.

In his picture, the hole extends beyond the bottom of the page. It looks like it keeps going.

It can't keep going.

Everything has a bottom.

It's something Hickson believes. To know there is an end to things. At a certain point, boundaries. Things separate and divide.

So everything has conclusion.

Things don't just appear.

They have an origin.

Cause.

Hickson sits there and tries to think. He looks out the kitchen window and he can see, in the moonlight, the scaffolding of his shed.

When he first came back from the Gulf, things seemed good. Karen said that they were good. It was a blur then, what happened there. He'd received the Silver Star for his troubles. Hickson didn't need it. Being back was enough. Real showers. Real food. Many nights, he and Karen would lie in bed and talk.

Then one day, driving to the store, his heart started racing and he broke out in a sweat. He pulled to the side of the road and something about the noise or the trucks passing, it felt as though he would leap from his skin. He scooted across the cab, opened the passenger door, and began to retch.

The feeling passed. It looked, to Hickson, like it was just the one time. And then he was out with Karen, and he'd had, maybe, two and a half beers, and his eyes, of a sudden, began to twitch. The lights started to smear. They were sitting in a booth, laughing and chatting, and then something in Hickson separated, and he stood and walked from the room. He went outside. He thought he was passing. Karen was there by his shoulder, and she helped him to the pickup, and they never talked about the night again.

It got worse. Hickson couldn't sleep. Had no appetite. He couldn't stand to be touched. Karen, she'd want them to go do things, but Hickson didn't want to do things. He didn't want to be away from the house. She convinced him to see a doctor, and the doctor said he was having panic attacks. Anxiety. Depression.

He prescribed Lorazepam for Hickson. Xanax and Paxil.

The pills helped for a while.

Then they didn't.

He began to retreat. It was like watching the world recede. Karen would be at the end of the bed, trying to talk with him, and Hickson would sink further and further behind his eyes. If he spoke with her, it was like having to ascend a flight of stairs.

She said he needed to see someone, but Hickson wouldn't do that. He was done seeing people. He sat in his den with a ray of sunlight slanting across his leg and looked at the yard. He sat there and sat there, losing track of his days. He was thinking of desert. Heat and windburn and scorpions the size of crabs. Burning pumpjacks. Burning flesh.

And then he looked up one afternoon and she was standing in the doorway.

She said that she was done as well.

Karen left, and for two years, Hickson felt himself dropping. Parks was back by then, and the man would come over, bring him movies, beer. When Hickson attempts to recall the period, he can remember almost nothing. No conversations. Nothing you might hear or see or smell. A lost time. As if that section of his life had been clipped from the reel.

And then one morning he woke and stepped onto his mower and cut a fresh swath of grass. He plied the brakes and looked back, studying the lines and angles, the perfect trail behind him, the world sliced into a rhombus of living felt.

He sat staring at it.

Then he levered the mower into first.

He took a job at the golf course. He began to work in his yard. Crossing the greens, crossing his lawn, Hickson felt himself gradually balance. He felt, were he to stop moving, he would forever sink. It was not quite living and not quite dying. It was treading water to keep yourself afloat.

Staring out the window, Hickson thinks about that.

He walks over to his desk and computer, clicks the browser. He brings up a search engine and types the word *hole*. He puts in quotation marks. He takes them out. He types *underground, Oklahoma.* Types *tunnel*. Then he hits the GO button and scans the results. Four thousand three hundred fifty-eight entries. He scrolls down the computer screen. He begins to sift through.

He reads an article about drilling. He reads another about mines. He studies a website advertising tours through a cave in the northeastern part of the state. There are three of them a day.

He finds a piece about bootleggers in 1930s Tulsa. He reads about tunnels used to smuggle whiskey. There are T-shirts. There are pictures you can click on to enlarge.

Next he finds an entry about a child in a well, and next, one about the 1800s. He almost goes past it, when something catches his eye.

It's an article about Chinese immigrants employed by the railroads. How, in the 1890s, many were laid off and began to move east. Some went north to Chicago. Some down to Texas. A good number settled in Oklahoma City.

And then Hickson clicks the next page and finds that this community was not aboveground but below. In the 1950s, police officers escorted a health inspector and a few concerned business owners through an abandoned building, into the basement, and from there down a chute and into a vast network of rooms. The men reported an entire other city, thriving with commerce in a foreign tongue. Jokes were traded about holes and China, but the people here were real, and their city no joke. There were temples and shrines and burial places; markets, shops, entries to more tunnels that went to buildings in different parts of the city. Tunnels that went beyond the city limits. Tunnels that went no one knew where. The people down there spoke little English. They referred to police as *topsiders* and they were pretty much ignored.

Hickson reads and rereads the article. He does another search and finds websites corroborating the story. Pictures. Maps. He sits for a moment and leans back in his chair. One writer had speculated about other towns with underground cities, towns whose belowground inhabitants might outnumber those dwelling above.

Hickson sits and imagines these people. Men and women fleeing railroads or enslavement in mining facilities and camps. They'd cross the plains, build an establishment. They would look, to white settlers, like people from another world. They'd have to make themselves another world, dig into it from ghettos and slums. Maybe all manner of folk, not just the Chinese. The cast-out. The passed-over. They'd leave the earth above them and delve deeper. Find other ways of being. Find another life.

And there is admiration inside Hickson. For the resilience.

There is something else inside him.

Which is revulsion.

The throwing off of order. The decision to tunnel down. Hickson can understand its appeal. Having no options, how someone could do this.

But the sheer fact of chaos. The hollowing of territory. You walk on earth that is only a brittle shell. Miners have come from other lands to make it brittle. To make their way beneath you. Because of them, your life could collapse.

Hickson glances at the webpage and closes it. He turns off his computer, makes his way down the hall.

His mind is figuring the distance to Oklahoma City. As the crow flies, forty-seven miles.

He must remind himself what he's read is a story.

He knows nothing, as of yet.

Eleven o'clock Saturday morning, Hickson and Parks stand in front of Hickson's garage. They are barefoot and shirtless and both are staring at Hickson's truck.

The tires, this time, are intact, but across the front grille, and over the door panels, across the windshield and the driver's-side window and the rear window and blinkers, someone has scribbled, in black spray paint, alien designs. Curlicues. Asterisks. Letters in a back-slanted font. The number *13*.

"You have *got*," says Parks, "to fucking be kidding."

Hickson studies it a moment. He says it's J.T.

"Who?"

"Kid from my work."

"Mexican kid?"

"Half Mexican," says Hickson.

"What's the other half—Rottweiler?"

"Chickasaw."

"That'd do it."

The two of them stand there, Hickson staring at the pavement.

"Get in the truck," says Parks.

"What?"

"Get in," Parks says.

"Where we going?"

"Car wash."

"Won't work."

"Will too work. We're going to wash it off and wax it and we're going to clean out the garage and put your truck inside. Then you're going to show me where this hoodlum lives and we're going to break a bat over his head."

Hickson straightens. He looks down the street.

"C'mon," says Parks.

The man walks over, takes the keys from Hickson's belt, lets himself in the driver's-side door, and slides behind the wheel. He leans across the cab and opens the passenger door.

They take the black off the body with Windex and a mixture of ammonia and 409. They scrape it off the windows with a razor blade. They clean it from the mags with Goof Off and they clean it from the blinkers with pet shampoo and half a bottle of acrylic paint remover. They work till late in the evening and when they are finished, Hickson cannot tell his truck has been spray-painted at all. They spend two and a half hours clearing boxes out of the garage, reorganizing Hickson's workbench, and then pull the truck inside and close the door.

"Now," says Parks, "we turn off the lights and wait."

Hickson turns to ask what for, but Parks leaves him standing there and walks next door, and when he returns he has half a case of Budweiser, a sleeping bag, his service-issue .45, and a twelve-gauge sawed-off with a pistol grip. He moves the table from the front bay window, squats on the floor, and begins feeding shells into the belly of the gun. He looks up at Hickson. He reaches over and cracks the tab on a beer.

"What?" he asks Hickson. "What?"

A quiet night. A quiet Sunday. Hickson works Monday morning, making his rounds. Dresser is in Tucson, and no one has seen J.T. since the previous week. He calls Parks that afternoon and gives him an all-clear. The man is still sitting watch at Hickson's home.

"Been peaceful around here," Parks tells him, noise from the background like gunshots or mortars. "I got the rest of the shed up around noon."

"Appreciate that," says Hickson. He keeps hearing gunfire over the phone. He holds the cell away from his ear a moment and turns down the volume. The noise is still there when he brings it back. "What's that I'm hearing?" he asks. "That the TV?"

"No," Parks tells him, "PlayStation. I brought it over. I'm stuck on this— *Shit!*"

"What?"

"I'm taking fire from behind."

"Oh."

"Can I give you a call later?"

"Don't worry about it," Hickson says.

He pockets the phone and stands a moment at his bench. The summer after graduation, he and Parks entered the service. Their plan was to go Army Ranger. Special Forces. Parks even made jokes about Delta, but Hickson knew jokes were all. They'd won three state championships, two in football, one in track. Parks said it would be no problem. They made it to Fort Benning, and two weeks in, Parks twisted his ankle and was dropped on request. He shipped to an infantry battalion in Fort Riley, Kansas, and on Hickson went. He passed Mountain Phase, passed the Phase in Florida. He received a Ranger tab for his sleeve and a winged parachute over his left pocket. He was placed in cadre, and Saddam invaded, and his unit was deployed. They were in-country within the month. Parks went to Saudi, where he worked filing papers at Supply. His ankle had fractured in two places and he walked two years after with a limp. Hickson's war was a different color. It was tracer-orange and white phosphorus and night-vision green.

He thinks about this. Parks's dog tags, Parks's games.

Hickson has wished their positions reversed.

He spends the rest of the day repairing the carburetor on one of the gas-powered carts. He takes a trip around the course before sundown to make sure Williams has collected the flags.

He comes up the cart path by the fairway on Seven, the tree limbs stretched against the evening. Their leaves yellowed. Brown. In the east the sky has cleared, but clouds are piled on the horizon to the west, sunlight backing their edges. The air around him is a peculiar shade. It stands in a haze in the space between the trees and sits in a low fog in the hollows. Vapor. Pockets of mist. Hickson breathes it like some kind of smoke. He waves at it with his hand. He rounds a curve in the trail, looks back toward the creek, and just then J.T. steps from the tree line with a shovel and walks downfield.

Hickson slows the cart.

He stops.

He sits quietly, watching the boy. If J.T. has seen him, he doesn't show it in his stride. He moves at a deliberate pace, planting the blade of the shovel, using the implement like an oversized cane. There will be a path of sickle-shaped divots through the rough that Hickson will have to fix. He drags a thumb across his chin and eases his foot toward the accelerator. The boy continues walking. He steps across to a manhole just up from the creek and pries off the cover with the head of the spade. He tosses the shovel down inside, then squats, eases his legs into the hole, and then the rest of his body. In a few moments his head erupts and glances around. Then it vanishes.

Hickson watches. He looks at the rusted nub of the manhole against the tree line, and then over to the hill across the creek. His housing addition not a hundred yards away. He looks back and forth between the two, and something like a laugh escapes his lips.

"The son of a bitch," Hickson says.

That night, Martin lay with her, talking names. It was a game they'd played since the first trimester. They thought about buying one of those books, researching family history, but it was more fun just to talk. They'd go to sleep every night with a name in mind, wake the next day and start again.

It was around midnight and there was no moon. No starlight. Martin glanced out the window several times and he couldn't see the pond. It was just the sound of crickets and Deborah and the dark. Every now and then the thermostat would click and the heat would come on. It would run for a while, click off.

"Christopher," she suggested, her voice seeming to come from the mound of covers. "Christopher Jarrett."

"Jarrett?" said Martin

"Sure," she said. "I have a cousin named Jarrett."

"You have a cousin named Jarrett?"

"Yeah."

"I have a cousin named Aloysius."

She punched his shoulder. "You do not."

Martin shook his head.

"What about Jason?" she said.

"What about it?"

"It's nice."

"Christopher *Jason*?"

"No. Just Jason. Jason Martin. Jason Lee Martin. You'd have the same initials."

Martin rolled onto his side. "What's wrong with Christopher?" he said. "I thought Christopher was good."

She scooted closer to him. She placed the bottoms of her feet on his shin.

"Hey!" he said.

"Hey, what?"

"Cold."

She rubbed her feet back and forth across his calf. Then she moved them.

Martin snuck his arm beneath her head and pulled her onto his shoulder. "Bring them back."

"No," she said.

"Bring them back."

They lay there. He felt her feet on his shin again. Then she moved them up to his thigh.

"You're just going right for it," he said.

Deborah laughed.

"So," he said. "Jarrett Lee?"

"Yeah. Jarrett Lee."

"You don't like Christopher?"

"I like Jarrett."

Martin thought about it. Then he thought about the boy.

They lay there several minutes.

The heat clicked off.

"What's the matter?" she asked.

"Nothing," said Martin.

"What is it?"

"Nothing," Martin said.

She ran her hand back and forth across his chest. She told him everything would be all right. She told him nothing like that could happen again.

"How do you know?" Martin asked.

"I just do," she said. "You've had your thing. This is something else."

"Something else?"

"Yeah."

"Can't happen again?"

"It's like lightning."

Martin thought about that. The chance of the same thing twice. Of course, it would not be the same thing if their son was born dead, because the child she carried was not Peter and lightning could strike him just as easy.

He closed his eyes. He reached over and cupped Deborah's stomach with a palm. He thought a prayer, and that prayer was for his son not to be taken.

He opened his eyes and lay there. He turned his head and looked over to see if she was asleep.

She wasn't asleep.

She was watching.

"Shhhhhhhhhhhh," she said.

The story hit the papers. It hit the local news. There were leads and sightings and all of them false. People called in or emailed. Turned out they'd seen the wrong boy. Or no boy at all. They sat with friends and reported it as a prank. Martin threatened to have them arrested, but there just wasn't time. Every day they were searching abandoned buildings, dragging rivers, creeks, interviewing witnesses, friends, former teachers and schoolmates. A math instructor who called the boy a savant. A wrestling coach who said the boy could do anything he put his mind to. Said he was the finest athlete he'd trained. Said bar none. The man went on and on. Martin took notes on all of it. None of it seemed to help. Every day was one more that added toward an opinion that the boy had simply vanished. Or was dead.

Rumors were he was a gang member. That he'd been involved in a crime syndicate. That on his way to work he'd been abducted by a killer, one of the monsters you heard about on CNN. A man in a semi with a torture chamber in tow.

One story bled into another.

People rehearsed them more and more.

It was a week since the boy was reported missing. Then it was two weeks. Three. They were well into December and Perser was hit by an ice storm, and then it was hit by another. Schools were closed and power lines were down and the investigation halted, and then Christmas was upon them, and then the new year. Articles about the boy dwindled. Folks gave him up for a runaway, or an abductee, or a corpse. Martin kept looking. He kept in touch with the family and tribe, and each week he added material to the file. He added clippings and Post-its and he knew now he was the only one. He'd sit at his desk before driving home to Deborah, sit and stare at the picture the grandmother had given him. He'd sit slumped in his chair with the photograph cupped in his palms, and it was as if he were having a conversation. He imagined what the boy might think or say. He imagined his voice. He imagined him alive, smiling the same smile as the one that glinted from the photo.

Martin would mumble to it.

"Where are you?" he'd say.

At home, Deborah would ask about the boy. She'd ask what was wrong. The woman had never seen him like this and Martin tried to hide it. She seemed to catch him every time. Staring into space or sitting with his brow knotted or she'd have said something to him and he simply hadn't heard.

"Hey," she'd say, "just talk to me," and Martin did his best. He told about his brother and he told about J.T., how the two merged for him, seemed in some way to blend. They'd gotten mixed down inside him. They'd gotten swapped. Martin's attempts to separate them would always seem to fail. He could reason his way into dividing them, but his feelings couldn't be sorted.

"It's like it's happening all over. Some part of it won't quit."

They were sitting in the driveway one morning. He was going to take her to town. They'd been talking about the case and Martin was running through the facts. He'd pulled the car into reverse and his stomach made a hideous growl. Deborah looked at him.

"Jerry Martin," she said, "my sweet Lord."

The sheriff shook his head. He opened the door, leaned out a bit, and spat bile on the gravel, bile mixed with blood. Deborah unbuckled her seat belt and slid across the seat.

"Are you all right?"

"I'm okay."

"You don't look okay."

"I'll make it," he said.

Deborah put a hand to his shoulder.

"This is making you sick," she said.

Martin sat there.

"You're going to get ulcers."

"I think," he told her, "they're already here."

Work went on. There were new duties and crimes. Martin attended court and served warrants and transferred prisoners from one cell to another while the county was repainting. He worked an arson case that January, the usual post-holiday domestics, gave speeding tickets, accompanied his deputies on a drug bust east of town. He helped a rancher corral this skinny calf which had gotten somehow through the barbed-wire fence and onto the shoulder of the highway. The sheriff stood there in the failing winter light, arms spread, herding the animal back toward the gravel drive.

Then February came and the baby was due and one afternoon when Martin got in from lunch, a call came over the radio from Lem. The deputy was at the golf course where someone reported a smell around the tee box off Nine, and Lemming had ended up going down the manhole to check. He'd found a body, terribly decomposed.

"Sheriff," he said, "someone beat him just to mush."

Martin sat, listening. He thought of the grandmother. Of ascending those stairs. He asked Lem had anyone told the family.

Lem asked him what he meant.

"The family," Martin repeated. "His grandmama and aunt. You ought not have to hear something like that over the—"

"Sheriff," he said, "this ain't no teenager."

"What's that?"

"This ain't J.T."

"Not J.T.?"

"Uh-uh," Lemming told him. "Guy I found, he's a full-grown man."

Martin sat there. He'd heard what his deputy said, but he told him ten-nine, repeat transmission.

Then he told him to repeat it again.

THOMAS SPEAKS

And so I started to tempt Him. To take me. Kill me. Drag me down, destroy me. You know the word. Et cetera.

I dropped school. I just one day quit going. Nana, you could tell it upset her. You could tell it hurt Aunt Angelica.

But here's the thing. About hurting people.

I have this meter inside me. I try and do what I can. I'm nervous and my stomach hurts. I vomit lumps of blood. It'll be that way for months. Trying to hold it. Trying to keep it down. And then it's like a lever breaking and everything floods, and I can feel it happening—I'm not nervous at all then—and all the time I'm thinking: Well, I hope everyone can just stay out of the way.

Nana knows it. Angelica, she knows it too. They didn't even fuss. About my quitting. Deciding not to go to school. And by the end of that week, I'd gotten a job. I knew I'd have to have one. It took some thinking trying to figure what.

I needed something to where I could be outside. Close to woods. I needed something where they'd leave me all alone. I was thinking about this, cutting across the golf course on my way into town. I'd just hopped the fence and I was going along the cart path by the lake, and I looked across the field and saw the greenskeeper changing cups. It was Mr. Hickson, but I didn't know him then. He was just a man. I watched him screw the cup-puncher into the green, pull out a tube of earth. He got back in his cart, went up the hill, and when he got gone I walked over and stood. The hole he left behind him was a perfect kind of hole. I'd never seen one close. I bent to touch it, ran my fingers along the rim. The dirt inside was cool and moist. The grass was moist.

I looked toward the clubhouse.

Then I started up the path.

They hired me on, forty hours a week. Making minimum. I was Chickasaw, and that meant part of my salary should've come from the tribe. They paid me off-book, though. I think Mr. Dresser had something going. The check he'd write me was his own personal check. Still a lot of money. For me it was a lot. Plus, it wasn't the paycheck I wanted.

It was Him.

I'd been there a few months, when I started looking. I didn't know what I'd find. I'd have to water, change the cups, mow in the evenings. Weed-eat. Trim the hedges. I'd have to sometimes shovel gravel, rake it into paths. And when the day was over, I'd punch my time card and cut across the course.

It'd be, by that time, just about dark. In fall, the whippoorwills. In spring, cicadas. I'd go down the path by Twelve, over-hill by the creek. You could stand and see Mr. Enoch's house just on the other side. The same pink stone as the building downtown.

I'd walk out to the green there, turn and watch the last of the sun. It would be sinking behind the park and the sky would be turning. Stars set inside the blue. You could look at them and feel the light on your skin. Feel it turning. It would get a little bit darker and a little bit darker, and I'd close my eyes and think of Shampe. I'd have my back to the creek and woods, and it was like I'd have Him pictured coming from the earth there, seeping up like a fog, and in my mind He was coming to take me. That feeling of watching stars in the evening and knowing if you were another person how good it would feel, and the sadness of knowing you'll never be that person, only the person you are.

Shampe was the answer to that. It's what Mr. Enoch had said but he'd never needed to say it. The story was all that it took.

It became, with me, almost a game. I'd stand there with my back turned. Eyes closed. Head tilted. Waiting for him to fetch me. Come up and take me. I'd wait some nights for nearly an hour. I'd stand until the thing inside me rose up and burst, and then there'd be the empty feeling, and it would be okay, and I'd make the walk home in the nighttime, and feel like I'd found something. Or lost something. Which in this kind of way I had. Spring and fall and winter. On into the next spring. The year turning from hot to cold.

But, like I've said, whenever I start out to get something, or lose something, there's always a thing I get or lose, I didn't expect.

Because—I need to say this—now we come to Shampe. A fact about Shampe. Which is: He never came. Never showed. Left me standing. Always just the waiting.

And so as the waiting seemed the thing—not even Shampe, you understand me, but waiting for Him, the trust—I needed something. To help me wait. What do they say? "Pass the time." Obvious, of course, what the pastime would be.

Think of it like this:

You open your eyes from standing and it is night and you're not taken. He hasn't erased you. You still exist. You're standing on a green with your back to the creek, and the close-mown grass is like a carpet, and over there's the hole.

Over the creek is Mr. Enoch's.

Just up the path, the shop.

No supervision.

No one looking.

Think about it.

What would you have done?

They park at the far side of the employee lot, close the truck doors quietly, and go across the blacktop toward the cart barn at a trot, half ducking, moving like the soldiers they once were. It is thick dusk and the sky has cleared. The evening's first stars Morse a cold, quiet light. Hickson and Parks make the aluminum barn, and Hickson unlocks a side door and lets them inside.

Dark black. The smell of must. Hickson comes up with a flashlight and leads them along the rows of carts. He selects one nearest the door, trips the hinge from the opener, and raises it. He and Parks climb into the cart, and he backs out of the garage, pulls around, and goes down the path.

"Remember," says Hickson, "it's just to scare him."

"I remember," Parks says.

Night is setting under the trees, in the depressions of the course, over the lake. The cart moves with its hushed electric whine, rocks popping under the tires, the rattle of clubs against one another in the back. Dresser's spare set. His cart. A row of golf balls rattle back and forth in the passenger-side cubby. They round a curve and Hickson points toward them, and Parks begins to load them one by one into the pockets of his shorts. They cross a bridge and then they cross another. The geese are gathered near the shore of the lake. They move among one another and spread their wings and hiss.

There is no wind. Not a ripple on the pond. Hickson pulls the cart by the sand trap on Six, sets the brake, removes the key. He gestures toward the tree line and then his boots are in the grass, and he is bent over, jogging. He makes it halfway to the woods and then he looks back. Parks is standing in back of the cart. Hickson drops to a knee and watches. The man's thin form is growing darker, blurred, and then it ducks and begins moving his way. He has a golf club in hand. A driver.

"The hell," Hickson asks him, "you going to do with that?"

Parks studies the three-wood as if considering the question. He looks at Hickson and shrugs.

The two of them reach the stand of oaks that run along the edge of the creek and work their way in and out of the trees until they come to the manhole where Hickson saw J.T. disappear. The metal lip of the hole is rusted and the lid cover lies upside down beside it. Parks and Hickson crouch at its edge and glance about. Hickson retrieves the flashlight from his pocket and peers inside. About ten feet down, concrete. A tunnel leading toward the stream. Hickson points at it and then over toward the woods.

"This drains into the creek. It branches into the storm drains off Nine and Six."

"And he was down here with a shovel?" asks Parks.

"It's how he got the lid off."

Parks shakes his head. He looks toward the hill across the creek.

"Your house isn't but, what? Hundred and fifty yards?"

"That's right," says Hickson.

"And you think he tunneled it?"

"What do you think?" Hickson asks.

They stare at the hole a few more minutes. They put the lid back on it and then look around them and stand. They have started back toward the cart when they hear a sharp report from the fairway to their left.

"The fuck is that?" says Parks.

The sound comes again.

It comes another time.

A third.

"Jesus," says Hickson. "It's somebody hitting balls."

The two men go back toward the tree line and then, traveling deeper into the woods, follow the sounds up-creek. Hickson walks point, ducking tree limbs, holding the larger branches lest they catch Parks across the face. He walks through spider webs. He walks them into a stand of pine. The thwack of the golf swings comes louder, and Hickson leads them back to the fairway. They crouch behind an ancient elm and peer out. To their right, a small form stands composed over a tee which the two men can only imagine. The arms trail back, the shoulders and hips, and then the silver shaft extending from the boy's hands whips to center and comes to rest above the left shoulder. The boy stands there, staring downfield. He bends, plants his tee, and reaching into a bucket behind him, sets another ball.

Hickson looks over at Parks.

He asks what planet they're on.

"Got me," Parks whispers. "Woke up this morning, could've sworn it was Earth."

Hickson shushes him. The boy drives another ball. Good form. Smooth and clean. Hickson shuts his eyes a moment, tries to help them better adjust. He looks just to the side of the boy to see him better in the light. J.T. sets up, hits again, and Hickson looks down the fairway, trying to reckon how far. He has a fine swing, no question. Hickson eases onto his knees and sits there watching. The moon appears low on the horizon, squatting like a pustule, yellow and full. The boy is backlit now. Brighter. That white shirt with its hem at his knees. The same cotton shorts. High-top sneakers. No telling what his swing would be in cleats.

J.T. strikes another ball. The moon rises brighter. Hickson can see a pair of headphones plugged into his ears.

"Hey," whispers Hickson, and then glances beside him to find Parks gone. He looks toward the trees and the sound of the creek. He stares several minutes into the dark. His friend was just at his elbow, crouching with the driver in hand. Hickson could feel his breath against the back of his neck. He strains his eyes. Curses. He starts to go look for him, and then, turning, pauses to watch J.T. There is the composure in his shoulders of a professional. That thing you can't teach. He's heard Dave say you can't teach it. He never would've thought it in the boy. He doesn't, he thinks, even see it in Dresser, and he is thinking about that when the boy tees again, and while he's bending to set another ball, a streak of white blurs past his head. Fifteen, sixteen feet above it. The boy doesn't seem to notice. Hickson grips the tree in front of him and rises onto the balls of his feet. He doesn't know what's happening. Then he does know. He almost calls out. There is another streak of white. Then another. The boy can hear nothing with headphones, and he looks to be focusing his attention only in front of him and to his left. He launches a golf ball and another pale flash smears above his head. This last one, however, is closer, and it catches J.T.'s attention. He slackens his hold on the club and turns to look behind him. It is then that Hickson shouts, and there is another streak, lower this time, and then a hard, hollow thud. J.T.'s knees buckle and he crumples to the ground.

Then Hickson is out from behind the tree, running. He is standing over the boy, waving his arms. He looks down and then back up, and he kneels beside J.T. and slaps, a few times, at his face. Parks emerges from the dark, golf club still in his grip. He squats beside Hickson and stares at the boy. His arms are limp, his legs bent beneath him. A knot is forming just above his right ear, his temple gone convex, swelling. Hickson gives J.T. a brief shake. He puts a finger to his throat. Half a minute and he lays his ear flush against the boy's chest.

"What," says Parks, "is he out?"

"No," says Hickson. "Dead."

By the time Martin arrived, there was a crowd. He weaved around cars and snugged the cruiser in between two pickups. People moved down-course. They pointed and walked. Martin didn't know if someone had notified the paper, but he hoped not. Mullins would write another of his articles and things would be even worse. The sheriff sat a moment, switched off the ignition. He stepped out of the car, crossed the fairway, and went down the cart path at a jog.

He reached the green winded, ears stinging from the cold. There was a mass of people gathered around the storm drain. Some talking to each other in low voices. Some shaking their heads. The smell was terrible, sickly sweet. Martin fetched at his nose. He looked over and saw Dresser standing there with palms on his knees. The man would walk a few feet from the hole, stand doubled like that, look back behind him, then walk farther away. Martin watched a few moments and Dresser finally looked up.

His eyes were watering.

He was pale.

"Hickson," he said.

Martin went across to the manhole, folks parting to step out of his way. Lemming stood with hands on his hips. Expressionless. Martin walked up and they stared at one another. He asked the deputy how bad.

Lemming looked at something in the distance.

"Bad," he said.

Martin cleared his throat and stared at the hole. He glanced at the crowd. Lemming passed him the tin of autopsy salve and Martin opened it, hooked a bit on the tip of his index finger, swiped it beneath either nostril. He pulled a peppermint from his pocket, popped it onto his tongue, and then knelt beside the hole. He didn't want to go down there. It wasn't just the smell or the body. It wasn't a lot of things. It was one thing exactly and it had been with him for the last thirty years. The sheriff tried to think. There were twenty people behind him and all of them watching. His deputy. Dresser. Martin closed his eyes. He could feel sunlight on their lids, a breeze blowing across the lashes. He was about to stand and walk to the car, and then he put his legs in and found the rungs. He lowered himself inch by inch.

There was no wind in the tunnel, but it was colder, and even with the salve, the smell was unbearable. He stooped and began walking. He heard Lemming coming close behind. The tunnel veered to the right, sloped down at a steeper angle, and up ahead Martin could see the body. He went over next to it and sat on his heels.

The body was bloated. The chest cavity had burst the seams of the shirt and the belt around the waist made the corpse resemble a link of sausage. It was a man, you could plainly see, but other than that you could tell almost nothing. The insects had been at him and they'd picked off a good deal of flesh. There was no hair or skin.

No eyes.

Martin looked away. He took a twig from the concrete beside him and turned back to Lemming.

"You go through his pockets?"

"I went through his pockets."

"Anything?"

"Nothing," Lemming said.

They sat like that. The scent of it burrowed inside your head and forced you to squint. Martin blinked several times and looked back over and noticed that the man's skull had been fractured. There was a cavity above the right orbital the size of a half-dollar. You could see inside.

Martin backed a few feet and Lemming came forward. The sheriff put his palm against the wall. To steady himself. He'd begun to sweat of a sudden and he could feel the panic starting, everything crowding, edging him in. Lemming said something, asked him something, turned to look. Martin was halfway down the tunnel. The deputy called out, asked him to wait, but Martin was already moving toward the manhole cover. He was hunched over, stooped, crouching his way back along the passage, back toward the light.

In the clubhouse, they sat in front of Dresser's desk. The pro still had that bleached expression. He looked at Martin and then at Lemming and then at Martin once again.

"Give me," he told them, "a fucking break."

"Didn't say anything," the sheriff said.

Dresser slumped in his chair. He rested his chin on his chest and seemed to study them from beneath his brows. "You were thinking it."

"What were we thinking?" Lemming asked.

Martin lifted a hand.

"No," said Lemming, "I want to hear this. I want to hear him go ahead tell us what's in our head."

Martin scribbled a few lines on his notepad, clicked, then reclicked the pen. He'd recouped himself, calmed a bit. He sat there trying to think what would be next. He was going to have to contact the coroner. The OSBI. Things would go quickly up the escalating chain. He looked back at Dresser.

"What?" he said. "You want me to accuse you?"

"Go fuck yourself."

"That's the spirit," said Lemming. "That's real good."

Martin cleared his throat. He leaned forward.

"Listen," he said. "Neither of us thinks you had anything to do with this, but you might stop acting so goddamned inconvenienced. It's a man laying back in that—"

"You think I'm not sick about it?" said Dresser.

"I don't doubt you're sick about it," said Martin. "We're not here trying to—"

"He's been with us ten years."

"Hickson?"

"Yes."

"And you think it's him?"

"I know it's him," said Dresser. "Who else would it be?"

Martin raised his hands. He asked the man would he just back up.

"Back up to what?" Dresser asked.

"Back to the part where he quit you."

"What about it?"

"When was it?"

Dresser leaned forward in his chair, opened a drawer in his desk, and shuffled through some papers. He started to turn toward a file cabinet and then rolled his eyes as if the task were too much.

"I don't know," he said. "Start of December."

"This last year?"

"Yeah, this last year."

"And he just quit."

"Yes," said Dresser, snapping his fingers. "Just like that."

"And he didn't give you a reason?"

"No," Dresser told him, "he didn't. He just walked in that door and told me that's it."

"You try and stop him?"

"Hell, no, I didn't try and stop him. How the hell would I have stopped him?"

"You could've asked him why. You could've—"

"Could've," said Dresser, shaking his head. "*Could've.* He walks in, tells me he's quitting, turns around, and walks out the door. What am I going to do? Tackle him?"

Martin looked at him a few moments. He scribbled on his pad. "Why do you think he left?"

"I already told you why he left."

"Why's that?"

"I already told you."

"Tell me again."

"J.T.," Dresser said. "All of them."

"The kids he supervised?"

"Yeah."

"I thought you were their boss."

"I am their boss," said Dresser. "I'm all of their boss. I was Hickson's until he up and quit."

"And he was over J.T.?"

"Yes."

"Like in a managerial position?"

"Exactly in a managerial position. Exactly."

"I'm taking it J.T. didn't like him?"

"No," said Dresser, "what I been saying." He pointed to the doorway. He seemed to be gesturing to the course beyond the windows, beyond that, the town. "Hickson had to watch all of them. He took care of those greens like it was his own backyard. Fucking hoodlums ganged up and—"

"You think they did this?"

"You don't?"

"I don't think anything," said Martin. "We haven't even found the boy."

Dresser snorted. He slumped farther in the chair.

"Something funny?" Lemming asked him.

"You haven't found the boy."

"No," said Lemming.

"How 'bout that," Dresser said.

They pulled into Hickson's subdivision half a mile up the highway, turned onto Maple, and then Scrimshaw, and then into Hickson's drive. Martin killed the engine. He and Lem sat studying the house. The oaks lining the street were bare now, a tangle of black limbs against the sky. It was overcast. Cold. You could see red tile from the roof of the Malcoz Estate behind the row of trees. Martin radioed Nita their location, then hung up the receiver. He looked at Lemming and then stepped from the car.

They went up the cobblestone walkway and over to the front porch. There were weeds in the flower beds. Weeds in the yard.

"Home of a greenskeeper," said Martin.

"Used to be," Lemming said.

They came up the front walk and knocked on the doorjamb. As soon as Martin did it he was sorry. He tried the door handle, but it was locked, and he stepped over and glanced in a window. He could see, through the curtains, a small section of carpet. A plant. It was a ficus and it was healthy. They could live a long time. He checked another window, then motioned to Lem. They walked around the side of the house.

"You ready to contaminate a crime scene?" asked the sheriff.

"I was born ready," Lemming said.

There was an eight-foot privacy fence, and the gate was bolted. Martin tried to work the mechanism from outside. He glanced over and Lem was already squatting with his shoulder against the fence and his hands cupped to make a stirrup.

Martin placed his boot in Lem's palm and the man boosted him to the top. He got a good hold, got a leg over, let himself down to the grass on the other side. The gate was padlocked. Martin thought about breaking the lock and then he stared at Lemming through a gap between one of the wooden planks. The deputy gave a shrug, then jumped, grabbed at the fence, and hoisted himself up. Martin watched the boards quiver under the man's weight. Then his other leg was over and he climbed down. Martin nodded and they walked around the backyard.

A lean-to. Flower beds. The lawn slightly sloping, the grass immaculate, dead. There was a shed standing in the yard's center. There was a wheelbarrow leaned against its side. Martin went around and ascended the steps of the rear deck and walked over to the sliding glass door. He pulled on the handle and the door skated backward on its track.

"That," said Martin, "was luck."

They walked inside and stood. Television and recliner and sofa and shelves. Everything in order. Perfectly aligned. Martin glanced at the row of pictures along the wall. He called out and asked was anybody home. He walked into the kitchen and opened the refrigerator. No milk. No lunch meat or cheese. There was a small container of yogurt, but it didn't expire for three more days. He asked Lemming how long did yogurt last. Lemming didn't know. He began going through cabinets, inspecting the shelves. He couldn't find pasta. He couldn't find bread.

"What," he asked the deputy, "does this man eat?"

Lemming shook his head.

They walked around the house, looking through envelopes, bills. Martin walked to the telephone, picked up the receiver, and there was still a tone. He hit the redial button and there was ringing and then a voice said, "Lowe's."

Martin told the person wrong number. He motioned to Lem and they went down the hall.

In the master bedroom they stood next to the king-sized bed. Bare mattress. No blankets or sheets. They found the laundry room, but there was no bedding in the washer or dryer. They checked the linen closets: no bedding there either. Martin looked at Lemming and Lemming looked back at him.

"This make sense to you?" asked the sheriff.

"Not any I know about."

"Get Bunker out here," Martin told him. "Radio Nita. Have him do a knock-around. See did anyone hear anything."

"We'll get ahold of the buddy."

"Hickson's?"

"Yeah. Construction guy. Matt what's-his-name."

"Parks," Martin said.

They went into the garage and there was a pickup inside it. Martin walked in back of the truck and took down the license number. He let himself into the cab. There was a hole in the console where the radio should have been and the dial that operated the air-conditioning was hanging from a wire. The plastic cracked and a vent caved in. Martin sat. He rifled through the glove box, then through a cubby beneath the armrest. There were receipts for building materials and kerosene lanterns, receipts for lumber and rope. There was one for a pickaxe and one for an entrenching tool. There was another for three emergency chain ladders. You could fasten them to a windowsill and escape from a second or third floor.

Hickson's home didn't have a second or third floor. Martin passed the receipts to Lemming and the man shuffled through them.

"What was he building?" Martin asked.

"For the course, maybe?"

"For what on the course?"

"I don't know," Lemming said.

Martin took back the receipts, checked the dates. They all read December. The eighth, ninth, and thirteenth.

"Twenty-seven lanterns," said Martin. "Why would a golf course need lanterns?"

"People are funny," said Lemming.

"Yeah," said Martin. "They're worse than that."

They walked back in the house. Martin let himself onto the front porch, checked the mailbox, but it was empty. He thought he might have a box at the post office. He went inside, tripped the deadbolt, and then he and Lemming walked out the back. They went down the steps and started across the lawn, and then Martin looked over at the shed. He glanced at Lem and gestured toward the building with his chin.

Martin walked over and opened the door. He stuck his head inside, but the shed was empty, nothing at all on the plywood floor. He closed the door and they climbed the fence and got in the cruiser. He'd just started the engine and was turning to back down the drive when he caught something in his peripheral vision.

"You see that?" he asked.

"See what?" Lemming said.

"The curtain," Martin told him. "Right there."

"Move?"

"Look like it moved."

"You sure?"

Martin sat a few moments. He stared at the house.

"Maybe," said Lem, "you're a little weirded out."

"I am a lot weirded out," Martin said.

"You want to check it? We can go back in."

Martin sat with the car idling. He thought about the lanterns and rope. Then he shook his head and ran a hand across his face.

"No," he said. "It's been a long day."

"Yeah," Lemming said. "Day ain't over."

It takes them fifteen minutes to complete the three-minute trip. Hickson steadies his hands on the steering wheel and grips it tighter as he drives. It is past nine now and the highway fronting the subdivision is deserted but for Hickson's truck. He keeps glancing into the rearview mirror. He keeps turning around and looking in the bed. His heart feels like an engine. It hasn't felt that way in years.

"I don't know why you did that!" he's screaming. "What did you think you were trying to do?"

Parks sits beside him, gone, for the moment, mute. He still has the driver in his hands.

Hickson looks back and forth between Parks and the road. He misses the turnoff to his addition, catches the next crossover, hooks a U, and then comes back down the highway slow. He turns in by the sign that says *Summit Green*, makes his way past the speed bumps, drives down the cul de sac on one side of which sits his home. He pulls into the driveway. Hits the remote. The light comes on and the door begins to scroll upward on its track. Hickson and Parks look at each other. Hickson pulls inside the garage.

He hits the remote again and the door closes behind them. It is a few seconds before he kills the ignition. Exhaust rises about the windows on either side. He can smell it and feel it down in his stomach. His heart going like mad. His pulse. Hickson draws a knee to his chest and kicks the console with the heel of his boot. Pieces of radio pelt the cab, pieces of plastic. Hickson kicks again, and when he kicks a third time something gives way and his foot sinks into the dash and gets wedged down inside it. He rips it free, his boot trailing stereo cable, wire.

The two of them sit a moment.

"I never thought I'd hit him," Parks says.

Hickson glances over. He opens the door and steps out.

He walks to the lamp above his workbench, turns on the 45-watt bulb, and angles it toward the wall. He cannot get his breath. His torso feels constricted and there are prickles down the backs of his legs. Like a power surge or current. Hickson stands. His house will be gone. His job will be gone. His yard and the course and what's left of his life. Accessory to murder before the fact and after. There is no backing out. He will be locked in a cinderblock cell with gang signs scribbled on the walls in feces and ink. Someone twice his size and functionally illiterate. It will be war, morning, noon, and night. He presses his palms against both temples and he presses them very hard. He tries to breathe and think. One at a time. One breath at a time. One thought. He reaches over and from a pile of old newspapers selects several sheets, doubles them, fetches the duct tape from a drawer, and begins measuring one-foot strips, tearing the ends with his teeth. He takes the sheets of newsprint to the garage door, looks out the two elliptical windows, then spreads the pages, taping them down. He stands a moment looking at the bed of the truck. It will be worse the longer he waits, but he waits regardless. Then he cannot wait any longer; he cannot bear it; and he lifts the handle and lets down the tailgate. Parks watches him, leaning against the wheel well on the pickup's right side. In the bed, a five-foot bundle wrapped in a length of tarp. Hickson climbs into the truck and begins to unroll it.

"Don't do that," Parks tells him.

Hickson says to give him a hand.

He grabs the end of the tarp, pulls up, and Parks climbs into the bed of the truck and pushes against the body. The blue spread of vinyl unfurls, and at the edge, on his back, lies the boy.

His brown skin is paler. His lips are pale, his hands a light shade of blue. Hickson studies his forearms. The tops have an appearance of having just been waxed. All underneath, down to the crook of his elbow, his arms are a deep crimson. Hickson covers his nose. He glances up and sees Parks doing the same. He looks back down. The boy's face is turned toward him, his eyelids open. There is a distended lump just above his temple, an abrasion of the skin. The pupil of his right eye takes up the entire iris. A number of flies buzz around the body. A dark trickle runs onto his leg. The tarp is wet with urine, sweat.

"My sweet Jesus," says Parks, weeping.

"Shut up," Hickson tells him.

"My sweet precious God."

"Shut the fuck up," Hickson says.

Hickson climbs in back of the boy, turns his face, reaches, and underhooks both arms. He lifts him several feet, then lets him back down. He tells Parks they're going to have to roll him up.

They tuck a corner of the tarp under the body and Parks pushes against it while Hickson takes up the slack. He climbs out of the truck, grabs the duct tape, climbs back in, folds the ends of the tarp back onto the body as one would a tortilla, then runs the tape three or four times around. He has Parks pull on the top so he can pass the tape around the body's middle. This done, Hickson sits back onto a side panel of the truck bed. A dark fluid has settled into the reinforcement grooves.

"I was just trying to scare him," Parks says.

Hickson sits there, panting. He wipes a forearm across his face. He feels like striking Parks. He feels like wrapping him up with the boy. He can't do that. One of them is going to have to think.

"Get up," he tells him, "grab that end."

Parks at the foot, Hickson at the head, they scoot the body out of the bed of the truck and walk it, stagger-step, to the doorway leading into Hickson's house. They set it down and open the door. A cool blast of air strikes Hickson and sends a shiver across his flesh. They lift the body, walk it through the washroom, down the hallway, through the kitchen, then pause, again, while Hickson pulls the blinds away and slides back the door. They heft the tarp and walk onto the deck, Hickson turning and going backward now, backing slowly and taking the steps one at a time. They are on the lawn now and now at the shed. They lower the body and Parks steps over to the small aluminum structure and opens its doors. Hickson looks to the houses on either side of him, but the windows are dark and the only thing he hears is himself.

"Watch out," Parks tells him. "It doesn't have a floor."

Hickson feels around and fetches up the ends of the tape. He pulls away each strip and rolls them into a ball. He grabs the tarp and rolls the body out of it. A muscle on the side of his back begins to spasm and then the spasm dies and he kneels there, sweating. Hickson reaches over and takes the boy's heels.

"On three," he says.

Hickson counts, and Parks takes up the arms of the corpse, and then he draws his hands back as if bitten. He walks over to the side of Hickson's house and begins to retch. Hickson stares at him a moment. He starts to say something, but there is nothing to say. He moves over and half lifts, half drags the boy into the shed, to the edge of the hole. Looking back, he sees Parks leaning with his palms against the side of the house, heaving.

Hickson puts his fists into the boy's back and pushes. The body slides across the grass, tumbles on itself, the T-shirt dragging. Hickson shoves harder and the body slips over the edge, and there is a wet sound, and then no sound, but his panting, and the flies.

Outside town, there is a superstore. Twenty-four hours. It is 1:58 in the morning. Parks and Hickson are walking the aisles.

Hickson pushes a cart in front of him. Parks walks along at his left. They are passing Automotive. Kitchen Supplies is just up and to the right. Inside the cart is a bottle of ammonia, fifty-five ounces; a case of paper towels. There is a windshield scraper and a new length of garden hose, two bottles of rubbing alcohol, a case of industrial-strength air freshener, a can of insecticide, several rolls of flying-insect tape. Hickson selects three or four terrycloth hand towels, burgundy in color, then a couple packages of aluminum foil. He buys a new flashlight. He buys a box of D-sized batteries. He buys a roll of plastic sheeting, garbage bags. He buys a bottle of Pine-Sol and then they make their way toward the front.

"What do you think?" Parks whispers.

Hickson shakes his head.

At this hour, crates of boxes line the aisles. Hickson must maneuver the cart between them. He pays for his purchases in cash, one hundred eighty-five and sixteen, all totaled, and then pushes the cart to the truck. The mags are still wet from the car wash and when Hickson lowers the tailgate, several streams of water leak from the bed.

They drive back to Hickson's, spend the next two hours cleaning, and then Hickson says that they should sleep. He lies atop the covers in the center of his bed and in half an hour he can hear Parks snoring. He walks into the living room and watches the man on the couch. Face upturned. Mouth open. His brow slackened and his wrists pulled to his chest and pressed together like a child's. Hickson stares a moment. He slides the glass door open and steps outside.

Early morning and the sky is caught between daylight and dark. Hickson stands in the grass and studies the shed. He walks over and opens the door. There is a creak to its hinges that he will have to grease. He steps inside and pulls the door to behind him.

Hickson kneels on the grass. He muffles the head of the flashlight he is carrying and then turns it on. His hand glows red against the bulb. He aims the beam down the hole, leans over, and looks. Dirt for as far as he can see. Motes swirling in the shaft of yellow light. He clicks the flashlight off, rises to his feet, and goes back out the door.

He sits, for a while, at the edge of the porch. Tries to think about options. With every option, there is the face of the boy spread prone on the tarp. Hickson sits there rubbing his palm back and forth across his scalp. If he goes to the police, they might make him a deal. Manslaughter, maybe. Reckless endangerment. He can't be responsible. All he did was put him down the hole. It was a hole the boy had dug for himself. Hickson looks at the shed and wishes he hadn't done it. That he could climb down some way, retrieve the body, bring it back up.

He sits a moment. Perhaps he'll get in the truck, drive to the courthouse, inform the sheriff. He looks over and he can see, through the glass door, Parks lying there on his couch. Hickson stands. He starts to walk across the deck, go back through the door, grab his keys, and get going, but something old encroaches, and he finds he cannot. *Surrender* is not a Ranger word. He sits back down and he can't decide if it's protecting his friend or protecting himself. Fear of police or fear of prison. He'll go, in the space of a moment, from hero to monster. Worst kind of monster. The killer of a child. Whatever the case, he'll do time. He knows what they do to child-killers in prison. They won't care he didn't swing the club. Everything in his life will be chaos and noise.

Hickson won't take that.

He knows that would be the end.

They didn't mean, he thinks, to do what they did. It was J.T. who had vandalized; J.T. who'd provoked them; J.T. who'd dug the hole. It could just as easily have gone the other way. He or Parks could have fallen in. Who, after all, was under attack?

It was Hickson.

It was Parks.

And thinking this, Hickson realizes. The problem is not the problem of *should-have-been*. The problem is the problem of *now*. It's not fantasy. It's not some other time. The boy is dead, his body gone, there isn't any bringing him back. Hickson can ruin two more lives. He can wreck them over an accident, or he can use what his country taught him.

He can stand up, dig in, defend what's left.

Or he can decide to give up.

Go under.

There isn't, when he thinks of it, much of a choice.

The tunnels are lit by torchlight, candles. The walls are of clay, clay packed beneath his feet, clay ceilings tapered and flickering in the flare of his torch. He holds one in his right hand and then he doesn't. He is barefoot and he pads his way down the channel encountering, every several yards, hardwood braces embedded in the walls. He stops and runs a hand over them. The lumber is smooth to the touch, oily, almost teaked. There are thousands of bottle caps pressed into the hallway, rusting and dented, murals of some kind, portraits. He presses his fingertips against them and through the metal he can feel the vibration of voices, a tin can murmur that grows louder the farther he goes. The path widens. The walls extend. He passes branches that lead to the left and the right. He stays his course and continues walking.

The tunnel broadens into a low-ceilinged room. Around the walls, like a Byzantine mosaic, broken bits of glass. Green and brown, all sizes. Bottle necks and bases, shards of window, fragments of jar. The light plays off a million serrated angles. The chamber smells of coal oil and clove. There are strings of white between the patterns of glass, enamel fault lines. They give back a curious gleam. He walks closer. Careful of the glass, he reaches out to touch one of the ivory threads. It is composed of pebble-sized marbles, but it seems they are not marbles. They are teeth. Human molars. Incisors. The teeth of rabbits and dogs. He retreats a few steps, and then slowly he turns. In the hall's center, a hole opens in the floor. Symmetrical. Perfectly round. He skirts its edge, walks to the far side of the room, then comes back, crouching on his elbows and knees. He approaches the hole a centimeter at a time, clenching shut his eyes. He is on his forearms and shins; he is on his stomach. He leans his head over the rim and feels a breeze against his face. He opens one eye. Then the other. He awakens reversed in bed, head to footboard, vomiting.

They drove east toward the town of Wewoka, this time to retrieve Ramrod from his home. The boy they called Ramrod. His real name was Herring. Dresser claimed the teens were responsible, and Martin thought he could be right. That he'd missed something. It was painful to think, but he had to think it. It's what people would remember, that he'd let a murderer walk among them. Any good he'd done would be forgotten. A high standard and a hard one, but Martin thought it was correct. He would've had the same reaction if positions were reversed.

They turned off 270 and took the lake road south. The last time they'd driven this way, leaves were falling. In several weeks they'd be coming back. Martin looked out his window and then he looked out Lem's. The sun was bright and the oak limbs hanging across the road webbed it with shadow. Shadows crossed his deputy's face.

He thought if he was wrong about Charles, about Chris and J.T., if they were perpetrators and not victims; if a man died because of his mistake; if he, through sheer blindness, allowed such a thing to happen—Martin didn't know. How you could take responsibility for such a thing. You could say you took responsibility, but what would that mean? *My fault*, you could say, and there would still be a corpse laid prone on its slab. There would still be the family grieving. An official could step forward and say it was on him, but that would only be partly the case. His office was a political office, but Martin couldn't think of it that way. What it amounted to was real people, real lives, not your presentation to a reporter or a jury. It was how he'd spent his time as sheriff and it was how he'd continue to spend it, whether it got him reelected or whether it got him fired. Martin shook his head. It didn't revive Hickson. It didn't put eyes in his sockets or skin onto his bones.

Up ahead was the clearing where the Herrings had their trailer. Martin slowed and pulled in. He thought he'd have to go through the routine of knocking and waiting, but the boy was out in the yard with the doors of his Camaro sprung open, cleaning the carpet. The hood was up and the trunk was up, and he had an extension cord running from the trailer, connected to a hand-vac. When Martin stepped from the car, the boy turned off the appliance. He sat it down in the grass. He took a rag from his pocket, wiped his hands, stared at the sheriff and his deputy a moment, and then he turned and began to run.

"Shit," Martin said.

Ramrod was seventeen and skinny and he looked very fast. Martin chased after him. He'd played basketball in high school, but that was a quarter of a century ago, and now he followed Lem, huffing. The deputy hadn't even broken a sweat. His expression hadn't changed. He outstripped Martin and Martin was trying hard to keep up. He couldn't. The boy made the tree line and then scrambled through the brush. Lemming was ahead of the sheriff, ten feet, twenty, and Martin tramped across the field in his cowboy boots, trying not to trip. He saw Lemming enter the woods and vanish. He clenched his teeth and ran.

By the time he reached the black oaks, he was winded. The ground sloped a hundred yards or so, then kept slanting down. Martin weaved himself among the branches and spider webs, gasping for air. He stopped and leaned against a pecan tree to catch his breath. The air smelled of wet wood. Smoke. Someone nearby burning his trash. It'd been a dry season and you weren't supposed to do that. Martin wondered should he stay here were the boy to slip Lemming and double back. Then he took his palms from the tree and began walking. He went downhill, breaking into a jog.

The ground fell sharply. It led to a creek. Martin could see it running below him, the waterline visible on the rocks just above. He picked a path down to the stream and started to look for a way up the opposite bank. He reached for his radio, but he'd left it in the car. He shook his head. He stood there, trying to listen.

Nothing but the sound of water.

Birdcalls.

The rustling of leaves.

Then Lem shouting his name.

Martin climbed the far bank and looked around. He began shuffling alongside the creek, calling back.

"Over here," said the deputy. "I'm down over here."

Martin ran along the creek bank, and then, right in front of him, there was a sink where a smaller stream trickled down and the ground fell sheer. It was a gulch, maybe eight feet across, fifteen deep. At the bottom, Lem straddled the boy. He looked up at Martin and waved.

The sheriff knelt.

"You all right?" he asked.

"Fast little booger," Lem panted.

"You get back up?"

"Yeah," the deputy said. He stood the boy to his feet—arms cuffed behind him—and walked him toward the creek. At water's edge, the narrow ravine opened. They crossed the creek bed and started back up the hill. The boy walked in front of them. All along one pants leg, the side of his shirt, his left arm and his face, there was a streak of wet clay. Martin thought he must have slid through it. It was an almost perfect swipe.

At the courthouse, Lemming cuffed the boy to the table in the room they used for interrogation. There were two chairs and the table and a window looking toward Main. There was a closed-circuit camera in the corner that ran to a twenty-inch television in the room adjoining. You could sit there and watch. A VCR would allow you to record. They didn't use the rooms often. Martin was pleased they didn't have to. He walked up the stairs with his coffee, crossed the room, passed the boy, then went over to the window. He stood awhile, watching late afternoon traffic. There was some sort of event down at the Lions Club, a cluster of vehicles along that side of the street.

The sheriff blew into his coffee.

"Why'd you run from us?" he asked.

"I don't know," said the boy.

"You don't know?"

"No," the boy told him. "I don't."

Martin turned and looked at him. He had straw-colored hair, pale skin. He'd taken off his sweatshirt and there was a tattoo on the inside of his right forearm, graffiti letters, so run together Martin couldn't read. He turned a little and then he could.

Ramrod, they said.

He shook his head. You'd get kids like this more and more. Farm kids, basically, pretending to be black. What they thought of as black. This amounted to what they thought of as *tough*, and tough, in Oklahoma, was currency of a special kind. In five years, the boy would be stealing, running crank. And if he lived long enough, he'd end up in the pen. There, in prison, he'd join the Aryans, and he'd emerge blaming culture for the waywardness of his youth. Martin saw it entirely too often. They didn't want to take responsibility. It wasn't, they decided, their fault. It was the Blacks, or the Indians, or the Immigrants, or the Feds. The Corporations. Oil Companies. The Ongoing War. It was everything. Anything. It made Martin sick.

"Do you know," he asked, "why you're under arrest?"

The boy looked up. " 'Cause I ran?"

"Right," Martin told him. "That's part of it."

"What's the rest?"

"Obstruction of justice."

"What's that?"

"That," said Martin, "means you're a liar. It means you're a sus-pect in a murder."

"What murder? Whose?"

"Hickson Crider."

"Who's that?"

"Greenskeeper at Hesston. He was J.T.'s boss."

"J.T.'s boss?"

"Yes."

"I don't know nothing about J.T.'s boss."

"Charles says you guys tagged him."

"Charlie is a lying sack of shit."

"You can tell him that," said Martin. "My deputy's on his way to pick him up."

The boy sat there. He shifted in the chair and then reached and scratched at his wrist. Martin studied him. He didn't look like a killer, but the sheriff had been wrong before. Teenage boys. They behaved differently in groups. He'd trusted Charles. Had a feeling about him. Hickson's death would be bad for people. A war hero. Decorated veteran. If Dresser started talking, and he most certainly would, Charles and Ramrod were going to have to be in protective custody. Whether they'd done anything or they hadn't.

"Come on," said Martin. "You need to tell me."

"I didn't kill nobody."

"Prove it."

"I can't prove it."

"Tell me about Hickson. You tag him?"

"Yeah," said Chris. "We tagged him."

"Why'd you do that?"

"J.T. wanted."

"You did Dresser too?"

"Yeah, we did Dresser."

"Dresser and Hickson?"

"Yeah."

"Because J.T. wanted?"

"Yeah."

"Why," asked Martin, "did J.T. want that?"

Chris dropped his head and shook it.

"I can't believe this," he said.

"What can't you believe?"

"This is America," the boy told him. "It was just a prank."

"America," said Martin. "Prank."

"Yeah. They were riding J.T. They were going to fire him. We just wanted to—"

"What?" said Martin.

"That's it," the boy said.

"You realize that's motive."

Chris fetched at his forehead.

He told Martin he didn't do it.

"Didn't do what?"

"Kill anybody."

Martin moved from the window and sat at the other side of the table. He asked what about J.T.

"J.T.," Chris blubbered.

"Go ahead."

"How do I get out of this?"

"Out of what?"

"This," the boy said.

"This interview?"

"Yeah."

"Tell the truth."

"I told you the truth."

"All of it?"

"All of it," the boy said.

"Why'd you kill Hickson?"

"I didn't kill Hickson."

"Why'd you kill J.T.?"

"I didn't kill anybody."

"Didn't kill anybody?"

"No," said the boy, "when's this over?"

"I told you when it's over."

At this, the boy collapsed onto the table and began to sob.

"I didn't do anything," he said. "I didn't. I didn't do anything. I didn't do it. I didn't. I didn't do anything. Don't I get to talk to somebody? I didn't kill anyone. Don't I get a lawyer?"

Martin stood. He felt old. Very tired. He slid his chair beneath the table and turned to walk out the door.

At this, the boy quit crying and glanced up.

"Where are you going?" he asked.

"Home," Martin said.

"What is it?" the boy asked him. "What'd I do?"

Martin turned in the doorway and looked back. "You said 'lawyer.'"

"Do I get one?"

"It's America," the sheriff said.

On his way home, the sheriff hooked a U and went back up the brick streets toward Main. He took a right and then he took another. He drove down the alley alongside the bank, pulled the cruiser into a narrow space beside the Dumpster, and parked.

He went down the sidewalk to the Malcoz Complex. He pitched his coffee into a nearby trash can and opened the door. The lettering read *Rick Bell, Attorney*, but Rick had been dead for a decade now. His partner had handled Martin's divorce. Before that the glass had read *Sheriff's Department*, and before that, something else. Martin closed the door behind him and crossed the foyer. There was a row of old mailboxes and Martin read the names and wondered how many of the people were still alive. He thought maybe none. The sheriff would be forty-five in August and that hadn't used to seem old. Something was changing. He went up the flight of stairs smelling that stale institutional odor he remembered from grade school, a scent like detergent and sweat. He reached the carpet at the top of the stairs and then went down the hallway, past doors with pebbled-glass windows, many still bearing names from the mailboxes below. Some were open. Martin could see bookshelves stacked with leather-bound volumes. Maps on the wood-paneled walls. He passed one room where there was survey equipment and then another where, on a walnut conference table, someone had built an elaborate scale model of Perser. The sheriff paused in the doorway to study it. The materials looked like the same materials used in railroad kits: miniature houses and trees, water tanks and buildings. Creek beds. Streets. There were even automobiles, figurines for tiny humans. The post office had been made of actual stone and there was an American flag the size of a paperclip flying from its dome. There were other flags on the model, larger, all black. They looked less like scenery and more like markers. The sheriff thought about the eccentricities of the rich. Then he thought *eccentric* didn't say it. He shook his head and started back down the hall.

At the sixth door on the left, *Matthew Gables* had been stenciled in an arch, and Martin paused here and knocked. He thought that much of his life as sheriff was knocking and waiting for folk to answer, wondering if they ever would.

The door opened and Enoch was standing there in the light of the tall windows. He waved Martin in. The old man was wearing jeans and boots and a western shirt and his hat rested on a nearby table. Martin didn't often see the man without it. His silver hair was parted down the center and pulled tightly into braids. The man pointed to a couple of rocking chairs that sat by the windows. You could see the street below, you could glance over and see the traffic. Across was the post office, people going up and down the marble steps. Martin went over and sat down and took his hat off and situated it on his knee. Enoch took the chair opposite. Martin had these things he was going to say and ask, but something about the view and the sunlight and Enoch sitting there beside him— Martin just sat for several minutes and rocked. Enoch sat beside him, rocking as well.

"I need to get one of these," Martin finally said.

Enoch nodded. He lifted his palm and gently slapped the chair's arm. "These," he said. "My grandfather made them."

Martin craned his neck and studied his chair. It was simple oak with a light varnish, but the workmanship was very fine and the frame felt sturdy and he noticed there were no nails used in its construction. It was all slat and peg. Something about that made a lot of sense to him, and something about that seemed impossible. That a man could design such a thing. Everything would fit together and it would perform as it was meant to and last for a very long time. He could hardly even fathom.

He stared out the window. He watched pigeons walk the edge of the buildings across the street. They had, maybe, an hour's worth of sun. He glanced over and looked at the wall of bookshelves. On a tattered towel lay one of the coyotes they'd rescued. When they'd first located the pups you could hold them in two palms. Enoch had found homes for the rest and the one that lay sleeping here had grown considerably. Its fur had lightened. Its snout elongated. The sheriff thought about tunneling down beneath the rocks that day to retrieve it.

"We found a body," he said.

Enoch didn't turn. His eyes were that very light shade of gray you sometimes see and his profile was edged with shadow. His lips were parted slightly. He rocked very slowly with both feet on the floor and just the toes of his boots flexing.

"In a manhole," continued Martin. "On the golf course. In the fairway off of Nine."

Enoch rocked. Martin thought he would ask if it was the boy, but he didn't. He didn't ask anything at all.

"Looks like a local," said Martin. "Hickson Crider."

Enoch nodded.

"You know Hickson? Lives in your subdivision?"

"I know him," Enoch said.

Martin watched the man. "They're going to come in," he said, "check dental records. Could be anybody."

"But you think it's him."

Martin was quiet a moment. He said it was him.

They sat rocking. Enoch mumbled his lips. He looked into his lap.

"I went down and saw him," Martin said.

The toes of Enoch's boots flexed, then flattened. Flexed, then flattened.

"I didn't want to go down there, but I did. I squatted there looking at him." Martin glanced out the window. He watched cars go up and down the street.

"And this man was killed?"

"Killed," Martin said.

"Murdered?"

"Most definitely murdered. There was a hole in his skull the size of your fist."

The old man nodded. His eyelids closed and opened. "And still we have the boy."

"The boy," Martin said. "He might be the one that did it."

"Did what?"

"Hickson."

They rocked and watched the fading light. The old man reached over and took an apple off the windowsill, quartered it with a pocketknife, and handed one of the slices to Martin.

Martin sat there, holding it in his hand. He hadn't eaten since morning and he didn't feel like eating now.

"Deborah's due any day," he said.

Enoch nodded. He placed one of the apple wedges in his mouth and chewed. He sat a few moments.

Then he said, "I lost my youngest son in Vietnam."

"I know," said Martin.

"I lost my oldest in Korea."

"I know," Martin said.

"The middle one missed both wars, and my wife and I were thankful."

"I didn't know you had another."

Enoch nodded. "He was a good boy. He was always good in school and he was in college at OU. Finance. He was going to go to work for the tribe. And then we got a call, Mary and I, and Richard had died. He'd been going to this well outside Norman, this little well on an oil lease he'd found. They had a pump came off the main line, had a processor, whathaveyou. Gasoline. What we used to call 'drip.' Rich had taken a blanket and he'd lain there with the nozzle off the pump breathing fumes. His roommate told us Rich would do this on weekends. He'd take that blanket and go out there by himself and just lie there, breathing. And then one weekend it was too much."

Martin sat there. He opened his mouth to say something. Then he closed it.

Enoch sat beside him and rocked.

"His mother and I," said the man, "we had three boys and all of them were taken. Jim and Daniel, people would say they knew what they were doing and had given their lives for something. Or there were others said the government had killed them and we should be angry. And with Richard, people would hear the story and they wouldn't have anything to say. They'd be sorry for us, and you could tell some of them thought we'd maybe done something for him to end up like that."

Enoch broke off. He seemed to be thinking.

"And maybe we did," he said. "Maybe there's things we didn't do and should've. I thought a lot about it. I know Mary thought about it and we talked of it until she got sick. I don't know why that happens."

Martin said he didn't either. He studied the man for a moment. He felt sorry for him and then he felt worried. He worried the same thing could happen to him and Deb.

"I had three sons," said Enoch, "and I lost them every one. I guess I thought of them, at one time, the way I thought of my books. And so what I have now are books. Stories. It's them I have to father now."

Martin thought about that. He looked back out the window. The pigeons stepped carefully. They staggered and pecked. They would walk the building's edge as if born to it. Then a car would go past, and they'd flutter into sky.

He'd just reached the highway when the radio started chirping. Martin picked up the receiver and told Nita to go ahead.

"Sheriff," she said.

"I'm here."

"Sheriff?"

"Yeah, Nita."

"Sheriff, we got a report on the body."

Martin pulled into the right lane and slowed. He hit his blinker. "How do you have a report? Coroner only picked him up a few hours ago."

"Well, he just faxed it from the hospital. Dental records. They're for a Matthew Parks. Lives over on Wallace. It's just across from Mr. Crider's—"

Martin told her he knew where it was. He pulled to the shoulder. He asked where was Lem.

"Last I talked to him, he was down in some woods."

"Get him," said Martin. "Have him meet me at Parks's."

"Sheriff," said Nita, "is there a problem?"

Martin checked his rearview mirror and then hooked a U and went back toward town.

He told Nita he was going to see.

Early morning and the sun is shrouded on the horizon's edge. Hickson stands in the fairway back of Nine, walking up and down, examining the grass. It has turned cooler and there is wind in the branches, leaves sailing steadily down. The sky is clouded. It spits an occasional drop of rain. The grass all around him is beaded with dew. Spider webs. The season's final green.

Hickson paces off thirty yards from the manhole, then steps into the woods and makes his way along the creek. He finds the elm they stood behind not twelve hours before and Hickson studies the ground all around it. The bark. He steps out from the trees and walks onto the fairway and searches the rough. Behind him, his footprints are damp ovals against the lighter field. He wanders back and forth, cuts here and there for sign. He finds nothing. He walks to the manhole and on the far side, every four feet, the just discernible chevrons where J.T. had planted his spade. Hickson bends down and studies them. He looks from the shovel marks to the manhole and he kneels for a very long time.

Later that morning, it begins to rain. Hickson sits behind the desk at the pro shop while a table of seniors puff cigarettes and talk. They are watching a game show on the television perched atop the vending machine and at every opportunity they slap each other and laugh. Hickson looks through the time cards. He finds the one with J.T.'s name scribbled across it and goes over the dates. The rain comes harder and begins to blow against the windows. The seniors consider it a moment and then turn back to their show. One of the men lights a pipe and bellows forth an enormous jet of smoke. Hickson watches. He shuffles the time card back into the pile. He glances out the window and a patrol car pulls into the parking lot. A deputy steps out. The sheriff. Hickson looks over at Dresser. Then he walks from behind the counter and goes down to his shed.

When he trips the lock that evening, Parks is standing in the foyer.

"You find it?" he asks.

"No," says Hickson.

"You think someone took it?"

"No," Hickson says.

They walk into the living room. Hickson sits in the recliner and Parks plants himself against the arm of the couch. He leans forward with elbows on his knees.

"You think it's still out there?"

"I know it's still out there."

"You think we can find it?"

"I don't know," Hickson says. "There's a thousand balls laying in those woods. It could've gone down the creek."

Parks listens attentively. At the end of every sentence he nods.

"How much blood you think is on it?"

Hickson says it's not the ball he's worried about. He tells him about the sheriff visiting that afternoon.

Midnight, they stand above the manhole. Hickson waves his

flashlight, then motions Parks forward. Parks kneels; wedges his crowbar; begins to pry off the lid.

The rain has stopped. Around them, in its place, falls a very fine mist. They wear slickers. Boots. Parks upends the manhole cover and it falls to the grass with a thump. Hickson shines his light down the hole.

"You first," Parks says.

Hickson crouches, puts his legs in, and sits on the rim. He looks up at Parks. The man turns his head. Hickson finds the ladder rungs with the toes of his boots, lowers himself, then eases down one step at a time. He strikes concrete, shines the flashlight around him, and then back up the hole.

"Fine," he says. "Come on down."

He keeps the beam trained on the ladder as Parks makes his descent, one hand gripping the crowbar, and then, bent double, they slowly make their way. They come to a turn and Hickson shines his light on a twelve-inch drain that snakes in from their left.

"That one," he says. "It branches in off Nine."

"The walls are cement," says Parks.

"Yeah," says Hickson.

"How'd he dig through cement?"

Hickson makes a hacking motion with his arms.

They round the corner and the passage widens and they walk side by side.

"Where's this go?" Parks asks.

Hickson gestures with the flashlight. "We're running toward the creek."

They walk twenty more feet and the tunnel begins to lighten. There is a pale sphere just ten yards ahead, a gray circle against the black. They hear the sound of water splashing, and then they come to the end of the channel, the water running over a concrete lip and falling into the creek bed below. Sand has collected at the opening, thatches of twig. There are steel bars spaced a foot or so apart. Trapped in the detritus, packed into the branches, there are balls. A hundred or more. J.T.'s shovel stands upright against the bars. They can see where the boy has burrowed into layers of silt. They can see where he has bent back two of the bars, just enough to slip through.

Hickson stares a moment. He tracks the flashlight over the sides of the tunnel, the concrete smooth and discolored, patches of algae, rust. He shakes his head.

"He wasn't down here digging."

"What was he doing?"

"He was getting balls."

"Balls?"

"Golf balls," Hickson says.

"Yeah," says Parks, "I know that. Why was he getting balls?"

Hickson sits there. He thinks about the boy's swing. He thinks about the composure in his stance. He has an image, in his mind, of the boy in sunlight, a crowd around him, watching him tee. They wait for his swing, watch the ball *swick* down the fairway. In a few moments they begin to clap.

Water streams over the concrete lip.

"The fuck were you thinking?" Hickson asks.

"You came and got me," Parks tells him. "*You* got *me*."

Hickson drops the flashlight and presses his palms against his eyes. Parks places a hand on Hickson's shoulder. The greenskeeper knocks it away.

"I wasn't trying to—"

"Shut up," says Hickson.

"I told you I—"

"Just shut up," Hickson says.

They sit several minutes. Finally, Hickson smoothes a hand across his face. He reaches, picks up the flashlight, and shines it down the tunnel behind them. With his thumb and index finger he pulls at the hair beneath his lower lip. He tugs, gently, the hair below his chin.

"I'm not going to prison," says Hickson.

Parks watches.

"I'm not going to prison, something like this."

Parks situates the crowbar on his lap.

"You hear me?"

Parks nods.

"You hear what I said?"

"Yes," Parks says.

They sit there. Hickson glances back and forth from the opening of the tunnel to the way they just came down.

"People die," says Hickson. "They get in accidents and you never hear word one about it. You know why you never hear about it?"

"Why?"

"Because they don't get caught. Because they don't let themselves get caught. Because they do what they have to not to get themselves caught."

Water continues running. Outside, it is beginning, once more, to rain.

"Fucking hole," says Parks.

"What?" asks Hickson.

"The hole."

"What about it?"

Parks points to the bars beside them, bent in the shape of parentheses. "He didn't dig it."

"No," says Hickson. "He did not."

They sit a long moment.

Parks begins to weep.

He tells Hickson he can't take it.

"Take what?" Hickson asks.

"This," Parks tells him.

"You're going to take it."

"I can't," says Parks. "I could call the sheriff, Hick. Say it was me. I could say that it was all on me."

Hickson studies his friend. He says that isn't going to work.

"Why not?"

"Because there's two of us."

"I know there's two of us."

"Good," says Hickson. "It's good that you know." He gestures back and forth between them. " 'Cause you fucked us both."

"I didn't mean to fuck us," says Parks.

"Doesn't matter."

"I can fix it."

"Calm down."

"I can tell them s'my fault."

"You need," says Hickson, "to shut your fucking mouth. Just shut your mouth and sit there. Just shut up and sit."

Parks crouches, glancing wildly.

"Can you do that?" Hickson asks him. "Can you go fucking calm?"

"I'm not like you," says Parks.

"Not like me."

"I'm not a killer," Parks says.

A moment passes. Hickson can feel his thoughts narrowing. He feels he is staring through a pin-sized hole.

"What'd you call me?" he asks.

Parks looks at him. There is a moment when the noise of the rain diminishes and the tunnel seems to go very bright. It looks like a photograph or still. Then he lifts the crowbar. He grips it in both hands and cocks it like a bat. The claw clangs a patch of metal embedded in the wall behind.

"Hickson," he says. "You stay the fuck away."

Hickson just stares. He knows Parks will strike him. He knows the man has turned. He's thinking how people switch on him. He's calculating the radius of the man's swing.

"I'm done," Parks tells him. "Want out of it. Just want to go home."

Hickson scoots forward a few inches, and then he scoots a few inches back. He feints with the flashlight, and Parks misses with his swing. Hickson traps the man's arm and pins the crowbar against the wall. He throws a hook to Parks's liver, another to his ribs, and then turns, flips him, and he is on top of the man, straddling his chest. Parks struggles beneath him and Hickson hits him in the face. He drops an elbow on the bridge of his nose and then twists the crowbar from the man's grip. Hickson takes it in both hands, and his heart is going, and he forces the rod of metal down on Parks's windpipe. The man's teeth part and his eyes widen and a harsh noise escapes his mouth.

"Home," he wheezes.

"You are home," Hickson says.

He waits until the garage door closes, then steps out and strips. He stands naked on the concrete floor, studying the knuckles of his hand. One of them is broken, but he can't say he feels it. What he feels is an energy buzzing his scalp, manic electricity. The hairs along his arms. Everything flexing. He stands a moment longer and then enters the house.

He walks into the living room. He walks down the hall. He goes into the bathroom and flips on the light. He stands there, studying himself in the mirror. Eyes bloodshot. Pupils swimming. He takes up his beard trimmer and unplugs it from the wall. Holds it in his palm. As if weighing it. Then he puts the guard on its lowest setting and runs it across his cheek. A thatch of blond hair falls to the counter. Hickson watches. He strips the other cheek, makes a pass above his lips. Across his chin. He smoothes everything, evens it up. The humming of the clipper connects to the humming in his head. His blood feels like some kind of fuel. He removes the guard from the shears and runs them across his scalp, along the back of his skull, above his ears.

He does it over and over.

He does it again.

When he's finished, all that remains is stubble. He leans closer to the mirror to inspect. He reaches up and taps his reflection. He taps it harder, raps it with a fist. He reaches in the shower, fetches up his razor. He turns on the tap and waits for the water to warm and then begins to lather his scalp.

Later, when he's seated in the den, something occurs to Hickson, and what occurs to him is that he has been here before. That was another time, another country, and it was the last occasion he remembers feeling well. He remembers looking out the open door of the helo, seeing the scrolling layers of sand dune, the red sand desert, and something about the wind on his face, his friends at either side of him, his hand palming the grip of an M4 rifle—all of this seemed like life. Karen would write him three times a week, and they were in a forward position, and in the afternoons they'd go to Sawbuck's tent and play games of checkers and chess. They bet socks, C-rations, dog tags, pictures of girlfriends, pictures of their wives.

He knew the officers above him, the enlisted men below, and he was a weapons sergeant, and he felt he had a place. A function. What they were doing was right. A lot of people said otherwise, but they didn't say that to him. At night he'd rendezvous with several troops from Marine recon, and they and three other Rangers would slip through the minefield, then across the border, navigate by GPS and the stars. The constellations seemed brighter there. The sky a little lower to the ground.

Hickson was tasked with walking point. He'd walk ahead ten or twelve meters, and every half klick they'd take a new bearing. They walked single file. To hide their numbers. To lessen the possibility of stepping on a mine. And it was even better, this walking at night. The silence and the stars. A short line of buddies behind him. His lungs big inside his chest.

Hickson thinks about this. He looks out the window and into the backyard sky. After he came home from the desert, it was like walking through mud. The air felt like mud. He slept too late in the morning and not well enough at night. Karen began to worry about him, and she said, one evening, he wasn't the same.

She was right. He was not. He couldn't ever remember feeling like he was. His sleep grew nightmare-fractured and his daytime, a haze. A fog of something. He'd sit at the table with her and it would be like seeing through mist. Walking through a mist. She seemed to go farther and farther, or he seemed to be dropping back, and then the distance was too much, and then she was gone.

Things were really bad then. He had to take it by the day. Sometimes, the hour. Parks came back from a furlough in Germany, bought the house behind him, and it was better, but it was still making do.

Hickson sits there. It doesn't feel like that now. He feels alert and watchful. Very awake. His thoughts now are different thoughts. Some other kind of thinking. It feels to him, suddenly, as if he is going to make it. There's just such a feeling. He can't even say.

They will be looking for him, thinks Hickson.

Let them fucking look.

He stands from the chair and walks to the window. He leans against it a moment, but he's having difficulty keeping still. He walks up the hall to the bedroom, and then he walks down the hall to the garage. He goes back and forth, pacing.

In the desert one night, they crossed the border and found a hide. Used their entrenching tools to dig in. They were to stay until evening of the following day, make their way back through the dark. It was a highway they were watching. Highway 80 linking Basra and Kuwait. Operations had just begun and Saddam was amassing troops at the border. Their orders were report on movement, count artillery, count vehicles and tanks. They set up at two in the morning, began digging their holes. One hundred and fifty miles inside enemy territory. February the twenty-third.

Pit Bull was their team leader. He was a large man and wore a size-sixteen boot. Hickson could remember following him. He'd step in the man's footprints and it was like a child placing his foot in his father's slipper. When they'd made their burrow that night, Pit Bull passed the other men and came back down the line. Hickson was lying on his stomach, watching the highway through his NVGs. Green and black and any light smeared with tracers. Pit Bull didn't like it. He didn't trust the coordinates. He thought they'd be too close to the highway, and there was a soccer goal about fifty yards across the dunes. It was their position, Pit Bull said, their orders, but he asked Hickson what he thought. Hickson had looked at the highway, and then back at his team leader. He glanced at the com officer, who was seated a few feet away from him, fetching at his dials. He asked Pit Bull what there was to like.

Dawn came like a fire on the horizon. You'd look up at the sky and hear the F-16s passing, making their runs, and sometimes the ground would quiver. Grains of sand dislodged and slid in front of him. The man next to Hickson, the com officer called Goddie, he lay there shaking his head. He'd been in Grenada, and then he'd been in Panama. He told Hickson he'd grown up as a Christian and he'd never planned on killing folks. Said when you first shot a man, it was a traumatic event, and Hickson had wondered why you would do it. He'd not killed anyone then, and he thought it would be just like the training. He thought Goddie had snuck past his superiors, that he was hiding something, that secretly he couldn't hack.

In an hour the sun was four hands off the horizon and trucks began to go past. Goddie was transmitting back to headquarters. Hickson and three others were keeping the count. The rest of them lay there sweating. Out on the road, trucks would stop and men would gather, some with black turbans and AK-47s and bandoliers of banana clips and grenades. Armed militia and townsfolk, readying themselves for a fight. Around noon, a bus stopped and an entire group of children in white garments unloaded and began to run about. They headed for the soccer goal and Hickson looked through his binoculars and someone had produced a ball. He looked down the line past the other men. He looked to Pit Bull. The man was shaking his head.

They lay watching the trucks. Some pulling tanks loaded on flatbeds. Some pulling trailers of light artillery. Hickson counted and watched the children. He knew what was going to happen. One errant kick and the ball would roll toward them and one of the boys would go chasing after it. He had a .380 with a threaded barrel and he'd just pulled it and screwed in the suppressor when the soccer ball lobbed into the air and came within twelve meters of their hide. And then three of the boys in their white robes and scarves. They were twenty meters away and then they were fifteen meters and then one of the children broke off, came down the slope of a dune, then up the rise below which Hickson and the men were hidden. The child stopped and looked back. The soccer ball was retrieved, the other two went back toward the field. *Go*, thought Hickson, *turn around, go*. The child ascended the rise and came walking toward them.

It was quiet. There was no breeze. All he could hear was a pair of sandals moving through sand. Hickson backed farther into the ground. Beside him, Goddie had flipped off the radio and unsheathed his knife. One scream from the child and it would be their eight rifles against a hundred.

Hickson flipped off the safety. He couldn't hear anything for a few moments. Then he glanced up and the child was standing right over him. Eyes wide. Mouth open. It was a young girl, maybe ten or eleven, and just as her chest expanded to release a shriek, Hickson grabbed her ankles and pulled her into the hide.

He cupped a hand over her mouth. He put the silencer against her left temple. He'd knocked the wind out of her and she was trying to recover her breath. Her arms were thin. She weighed almost nothing. She felt like some kind of bird. How he must have looked to her with his face streaked in muted colors of camo, all his gear and his weapons. The other men dug in beside him. Like monsters in the earth.

Hickson lay there, pinning her down. She had brown skin and dark features and one day, thought Hickson, she'd be very lovely. He wanted like hell not to have to shoot her. He looked down the line past Goddie, past the other men. He looked at Pit Bull. The man was blinking and looking back. In the middle was Roscoe, staff sergeant, Marine recon. The man was staring at Hickson. He kept tapping his temple and drawing an index finger across his throat. Hickson looked down at the girl. He tightened his hand against her mouth. He could feel the heat of breath from her nostrils, gasping for air. He was thinking of tying and gagging her when Goddie slapped him on the shoulder and pointed toward the road.

There was an irrigation ditch between their hide and the soccer goal. The children now were gone. They'd moved back to the bus. Hickson stuck the pistol in his belt, propped himself up, and looked through the binoculars. About a dozen of the men had left the main detachment and were walking right for them. Gesturing. Hickson stared a few moments and then looked back at the girl. He thought of Karen. What she'd say. He decided that, whatever happened, the girl would be all right. He would have to make sure.

F-16s were rocketing overhead. It was constant. Somewhere, up in the ether, was a plane designated to provide support. They'd not yet dropped their payload. They'd have plenty could help them

out. Goddie was radioing. He was apprising headquarters of the
dilemma. He'd send up the prayer and the gods would rain oblivion. Fire everywhere. The desert would erupt with it.

He looked down at the girl and he just had looked when a patch
of sand popped in front of Roscoe and the shot echoed through the
space back behind. Hickson hunkered. He took his hand off the
girl's mouth and unslung his rifle. He glanced over and saw Roscoe
elbow-walk forward, prop himself up, and take his first shot. Then
Sawbuck fired. Then two more of the men. Hickson looked downrange and saw that a couple of the Iraqis had fallen. He stared
through his scope, caught a man in his cross hairs, flipped off
the safety. He squeezed the trigger and a splash of red flew from
behind the man he'd sighted and the man went backward as if
kicked. Hickson felt his adrenaline go. He gritted his back teeth.
He looked over at Roscoe and saw the man smiling.

They fired more rounds. More rounds came back. A detachment of actual Iraqi troops had stopped at the roadside and one of
the militiamen was talking with the driver and pointing in their
direction. Three more trucks pulled in behind. Iraqi army. Hussein's Royal Guard. Pit Bull was staring through his binoculars and
he shook his head and motioned for them to fall back.

Hickson jerked the girl to her feet and began walking her
backward, using her as a shield. The air was hot. The sky so blue
it looked washed. Gunshots all around, ricochets. He went back
twenty yards, dropped to a knee, held position waiting for Goddie.
He was wiring the radio with C-4. They'd leave it behind, blow it.
They wouldn't have to hump it out. They were only a recon mission and they were carrying light ammo—M4s, sidearms, a few
RPGs. Roscoe had an MP5 he'd gotten God knew how. Hickson
knelt there, pressing the girl to the sand, holding the rifle upright
on a knee.

They fell back a hundred yards and then they fell back a hundred more. A few men topped the rise next to where they'd dug themselves in. The recon team fired and those men dropped as though weighted with brass. Goddie was fetching around for another radio. He'd lost the antennas on the spare in the rush to destroy equipment. All they had was a PRC-90. Goddie triggered it, crawled to Hickson, and began yelling.

They fired again and moved back. Fired and moved. The girl would huff breathlessly as they scooted and then, when they took position, begin hysterically to scream. Hickson smoothed his hand over the back of her head to calm her, but this only made it worse. Roscoe kept looking at him. He'd pop a few rounds and cast Hickson a glare. Hickson would shake his head. Idea was, if they lived through it, he'd leave the girl and maybe radio her position. He didn't know. "Shhhhhhhh," he told her, but the girl couldn't hear. They were firing like mad. Pockets of dust rose where rounds from the AKs would strike. They fell back farther, took posture on a rise, and that's when Goddie got through. He gave the pilots their coordinates and then the coordinates of their combatants. A minute later there was a streak in the sky, a loud crack, and then a line of concussions. Two hundred yards away, where the men came toward them, all that sector went up in flame. Hickson watched it through his scope. Iraqis were knocked prone. Some of them ablaze. Some disintegrated from the blast. Pit Bull gestured. They got back on the move.

They reached a kind of corridor, a bluff they'd come down the previous night. They'd have to make their way along a wall of rock, then across a dune in the open. They knelt down and set perimeter. Goddie was still on the radio. Hickson watched. The girl just sat with her eyes glazed, out of breath. Hickson looked over to Sawbuck and right then a pink mist erupted from his throat and he crumpled onto his face. He lay there like you'd bow for a prayer. Hickson moved toward him, but then they were taking fire. Roscoe was hit. Johnson was hit. He thought Pit Bull was hit, but he didn't know where. He pressed the girl to the ground and lay beside her, looking through his scope. Another detachment of troops were coming through the dunes.

It was the first time Hickson could remember being afraid. He knew he would die. Goddie was calling coordinates. The next set of fighters did a flyover and the man on the other end of the radio said they didn't have precision weaponry. They were carrying cluster bombs and the pilots couldn't guarantee the explosions wouldn't take Hickson's team as well. Hickson watched Goddie sit there. He turned around and told Pit Bull. You could see he was trying to think. Roscoe was backed to the wall of rock, one hand pressed to his side, bleeding through his fingers. The other holding his pistol. He was out of ammunition for his MP5. When he heard what Goddie told them he shook his head and swore. He struggled onto his feet and walked over to Hickson, and Hickson was about to tell him to get down, what was he doing, when the man bent and placed the barrel of his weapon to the girl's forehead and fired. She'd just turned to look behind her. And Roscoe took her away.

It was confusion. The men were bleeding and taking fire and Pit Bull gave the order for the 16s to drop ordnance. The enemy was close, you could see them crossing out there, maybe three hundred yards. They were firing and Goddie yelled for them to take cover. Hickson was still beside the girl, and he shouldered down into the sand and the first wave of bombs hit and it was like the earth would break.

Iraqis kept advancing. Pit Bull took a round through the leg. Sidney was shot three times in the chest. Roscoe was down beside Goddie helping him send through coordinates. They were calling in corrections and telling the pilots where to drop. Every time a wave of bombs came you'd have static and then the pilots asking, "Are you there?" Hickson couldn't believe it. He couldn't lie still.

Couldn't sit and stand it. He'd begun crying at some point but he hadn't noticed when. There were the shots they were taking, and the spray of sand against his face, the earth trembling, Goddie screaming numbers into the receiver. Hickson lay there, preparing himself to die.

He'd heard people talk like this. How they'd prepared themselves for death. How anyone could believe it, thought Hickson, even as joke. It wasn't a joke now. It was something else entirely. It was like part of him separated and went trailing off. He sat with his eyes closed, watching. That part which places stake in the next moment, the moment after. To think, now, there wouldn't be an after. Bombs were falling and sand was flaring up and there were great blasts that would suck oxygen out of the air and leave nothing it in its place. They couldn't live through it. The enemy would shoot them or their own bombs, probably, would send them to hell. Hickson tried to concede, just lie and wait it out. There would be a flash and then darkness. An end to his thoughts.

It was a hard thing for Hickson. He found he wasn't ready. His heart was still so full. Rage and grief and love. It was like you had to let go of all that, and you could release it only once. He lay curled in on himself, and in his mind he was in his boat with his grandfather and they were on the pond. Fishing lines trailed into the water and at their ends, bait. Hickson had a knife and he glanced at the old man and began to cut the cord. That one was Parks and that one was Karen and that one was bringing Roscoe up for court-martial, killing the girl. He moved about, cutting them. They kept you tethered to the world. Love and fear and hatred. Hickson severed them all. He severed them and then nodded to himself that he was ready. His heart was empty and he was ready, finally, to pass.

But he didn't pass. The 16s kept dropping closer, and the recon team shot up their ammo, and just after dark two Black Hawks came in to evacuate. They loaded three dead Rangers onto the plat-

form, and the remaining five climbed on aboard. In an hour they
were back in cadre, and the next week Hickson was awarded the
Silver Star. He and Pit Bull were given early release and he came
home August of that year. He'd pull out the medal and look at it,
and Karen, when she was here, she'd say she was proud.

Karen isn't here now. No one is but Hickson. And he knows
what he needs. To be moving. Out there, on the streets, they'd
catch up. He'll be arrested. Mexico or Canada, not even an option.
He'll be fine, he thinks, as long as there's movement. Parks's body
will be found, he wasn't strong enough to lift it. Eventually, they'll
come hunting.

He paces up the hallway and then paces back down. He walks
into the bathroom and on through the guest bedroom and then
he comes back and stands in the mirror, observing himself,
twitching.

It's like Karen once told him, before things had gotten bad.
They'd be seated at dinner, or maybe in a movie, and Hickson's
knee would begin to bounce. It would begin to quiver, begin trembling, and Hickson didn't even notice. Karen would look at him.
Clear her throat. He'd ask her what and she'd only shake her head.
She'd shake her head and reach over, try and steady his leg. She said
he was like a hummingbird. Said he was like a shark.

Keep flapping your wings.

Always keep swimming.

Stop moving just a second, you sink forever down.

Martin pulled into Parks's driveway and turned off his lights. He sat there a moment, trying to think. His heart was going and he could feel his blood beginning to hum. He unholstered his revolver, flipped out the cylinder, rotated it, checking the shells. He didn't know what he was checking for, but he did it regardless. He snapped the cylinder shut and studied the yard. The sagging gutters. Newspapers piled inside their miniature yellow sacks. He reckoned maybe sixty of them. Seventy. He shook his head and reholstered the weapon and stepped onto the pavement. Dusk was falling and he reached back inside and fetched up his flashlight, slid it in the metal ring on the back of his belt. Then he closed the door very quietly and stood in front of the house. There was a crow calling from down the street. The noise of a plane. Martin looked at the sky. Stars were just beginning to glint and then the sun dipped below the horizon. The heavens were a deep shade of purple. Martin walked across the lawn.

He stood for several minutes. He thought about knocking, but he didn't. He thought about waiting for Lem, but he didn't do that either. He went around the side of the house and found the gate. It'd been left slightly ajar and Martin opened it a few more inches and slid through. He peeked in a window. He squatted there and glanced about. He noticed the gate to Hickson's yard. He hadn't noticed it from the other side of the fence. It bothered him that he hadn't.

He walked over and opened it.

Then he went through.

The yard looked no different and there was no light from the house. He walked by the shed and up onto the deck, went over and slid back the door. He went inside and walked from room to room. He went to the ficus and pressed his fingers to the soil. Dry. He burrowed beneath the surface and about two inches down it grew moist. He squatted there, thinking. Then he exited the house and went down the back steps and over to the shed. He didn't feel right about it. He couldn't have said why. He pulled his pistol and curled a finger inside the trigger guard. He opened the door and peered inside. It was still empty. He closed the door and stood. He had a cold sensation at the back of his throat and he began, of a sudden, to sweat. He placed his palm on the handle and drew the shed's door open. From between the plywood panels that served as a floor there was a splinter of light. Martin studied it a few moments.

"Son of a bitch," he said.

He looked around for something with which to pry. He knelt in the grass and glanced behind him. Then he gripped his pistol in the other hand and unfolded his knife. He wedged the tip down inside the seam and began gently to lever it up. It came, no problem. Martin got a finger in. He worked in his hand. He took the panel and pulled it and then he just crouched there, blinking.

Under the panel was a hole. About three feet in diameter. From down inside it came a golden light. He almost dropped the plywood to reach for his radio, but he'd left it, once again, in the car.

He patted his pockets for his cell, but he didn't have that either. It occurred to him that any minute he'd be shot.

Martin licked his lips and glanced over either shoulder. He didn't really know who he was looking for, who avoiding. He closed his knife and clipped it back to his pocket, and then swapped the pistol to his right hand, holding the panel up with his left. He leaned farther and looked inside.

The hole went down four feet, and then there was another section of plywood, and then a tunnel angling off to the left. He could just see where a kerosene lantern hung from a length of twine. He pointed the gun toward the hole. Tried to think. If someone was in there, he'd be in there now. There was no other way Martin could think to set up the shed door and panel. You'd have to close both from inside. *Wait*, he thought. That wasn't right. You could close them from outside and just walk away. So he was either in the hole or he wasn't. He wasn't thinking clearly. He thought about going back to his car. Then he thought about someone being down there, that whoever was down there, Martin had him cornered. If he went back to the cruiser, whoever was down there, if he was down there, might come out. He'd come out, and know someone was looking, and he could slip over the fence, and that would be it. Another body vanished, someone else gone missing. Martin wondered could he live with it. There was no backup. No one to know exactly where he was. He looked from the shed over to where his cruiser would be, past the fence and house and yard. He touched his forehead to the grass and held it there a few moments. Deborah would not want him to do it. Martin thought about the boy.

He decided no. Too much of a risk. It wouldn't be procedure and if things went bad his office could be revoked. Deborah needed a husband. His son would need a father. All he had to do was walk to the cruiser, radio Nita, get ahold of Lem.

Martin let down the plywood panel and then stood and walked

back toward the gate. When he got to where he could no longer see the shed's entrance, he stopped and looked back. The small building standing there in the center of the yard. He would walk across and into the next lawn and he could imagine just then someone emerging from the tunnel, pushing his way up into the shed, out' its door, across the yard, over the fence. Then he'd be forever gone.

Martin stood there, a sick feeling in his stomach. It was his decision to make but he felt he'd already made it. Long ago, in the shallows of the Arkansas River. The sheriff wondered how that could be. He set his pistol at half cock and walked back to the shed.

He opened the door, lifted the panel, removed it, and positioned it on the grass.

Then he lifted out the other and stepped down inside.

He shutters the windows. He gathers supplies. He walks from room to room nodding to himself, muttering snatches of song. The next day he ventures out to buy lanterns. He buys a pickaxe and a chain ladder and thirty gallons of kerosene. He wakes in the afternoon just in time to see the sun declining. He stands there, watching out the window, running a palm across his scalp. The days are getting shorter. He doesn't have much time.

He spends most of his nights digging. He drives to Wal-Mart at three in the morning, purchases a tent. He doesn't want the tent, just the stakes, but they don't sell them separately. He glances over at the young man working Sporting Goods and the young man glances quickly away. He stares down at the counter. He doesn't look up. Hickson studies him. The tent is seventy dollars and he considers his bank account. Then he thinks of tunnels and then he doesn't care. Inside the shed, he lifts the plywood panels, stakes down the chain ladder, and lowers it into the hole. He buys an entrenching tool from the local Army surplus, and with this imple-ment in one hand, flashlight in the other, he descends a few feet. He descends a few more. It is warmer here, down in the earth. He looks back to the entrance and the ring of kerosene light. Then he wedges the flashlight in a rear pocket and begins to dig.

He starts by making the entrance to what will be his tunnel. There is the main shaft which appeared God knows how and which Hickson has ceased to consider. To consider as a problem. A collapsed well or whathaveyou, it serves now as escape route, his passage to a life below. He carves an opening in the side of the shaft, about four feet down, and he makes it wide enough to crawl in comfortably on his hands and knees. The earth crumbles away and in several hours he has produced a kind of shelf. He stakes off the chain ladder on the opposite side of the hole and digs out a notch into which he'll insert the platform, a plane of strong timber to block the shaft. The next night, he makes a trip to Lowe's, has an elderly woman cut down a sheet of two-inch plywood, and this he takes down into the hole. He wedges the square of wood in the notches he's dug, right next to the entrance to his tunnel. The plywood fits snugly, feels sturdy, and at each end there is a crescent-shaped gap between platform and burrow through which Hickson can sift the dirt. There is no need for the ladder now, and Hickson wakes later and later, drinks coffee, retreats to the shed, steps down into the hole and onto the plywood platform, enters his side tunnel, and begins digging. He buys two-by-fours to support the ceiling. He takes down a box of books from the attic, old books on Viet Cong miners, begins to study their scheme. He lays out maps. He draws new ones on sheets of graph paper. His vision seems to narrow and it is as if he's constructing another world.

He quits going to work. He quits returning calls. One evening, he drives to the pro shop, walks into Dresser's office, and tells the man he's finished. Dresser tries to talk Hickson out of it, but Hickson turns to leave. He has known Dave Dresser since fourth-grade history and this is the last he'll see of him.

It's the last he'll see of a number of things.

The tunnel gets longer. He goes farther into the earth. Every five feet he wedges a two-by-four against the ceiling as support. He hacks along and hits a sandstone formation, makes a dogleg, makes another. He's tunneled, by this point, perhaps a hundred yards and he hooks a U and begins tunneling back the way he came, tunneling adjacent to the first channel, always with a slope to it, always headed down.

It is at this time that Hickson begins to forget. It surprises him how quickly. It surprises him what.

He forgets recipes.

He forgets people's names.

He forgets holidays and presidents.

Movies and books.

Song titles.

Television series.

The date of his anniversary.

He forgets car parts. He forgets the parts of his guns. The first standing order of Rogers' Rangers is, *Don't forget nothing*, but he forgets the orders one by one. He forgets the Pledge of Allegiance and the words to the National Anthem. Reconnaissance Procedure. The Ranger Creed.

He begins forgetting events from his life. It is as if they are erased. His memory is an entrenching tool and a flashlight and lanterns dangling from lengths of twine, the buckets he fills and drags back to the entrance. There comes a day he cannot remember his mother's maiden name and then there comes a day when he cannot remember her first. He can remember the word *mother* and he can even remember to what the word refers. He digs farther and then this leaves him as well.

Late one night, dead of winter, he's lodged in the earth hacking away with a pick, when the soil gives way before him, pushes through and falls. He begins digging faster, pressing against the dirt, and discovers he has dug his way back to the original shaft, the one he discovered in his yard not three months before. It might as well be three centuries. Hickson pokes his head inside and glances up. Twenty feet above him is the platform he wedged blocking the hole, a faint light in the four half-moons along the edges. He sits there a moment and tries to think, but *thinking* is not exactly the word. He's changed down here, Hickson. Entered a new kind of state. Or reverted, perhaps. He doesn't seem to think in language. He thinks in image, in sound. He stays in motion, mostly, or he sleeps. He's begun sleeping in the earth, dragging his filthy bedding back behind him. He no longer takes his medication. He no longer dreams.

His nails have grown.

His hair and beard.

He crawls back and forth in his tunnel, relighting the lamps.

On rediscovery of the shaft, he pauses several days. Then he begins to dig around it. He hacks out a chamber, a room of sorts, pushing dirt and sandstone into the center, into the shaft. He's carved a kind of circle around it and day by day he makes it bigger, tall. He braces the ceiling with two-by-twelves and plywood planks. He tamps down the floor. There is his tunnel and now this room below. He can almost stand inside it. He brings down his food and blankets. He brings down canisters of fuel. He sits, through the day, with the lamps depending from pieces of twine, seated on the floor of his chamber, staring into the hole. Only October and he was twenty feet above, looking at it from his lawn. The lawn, now, is withered. Its caretaker underground. He cares now for his tunnel, cares for his room, and he is concerned, more and more, with this circle in its center. He throws in his refuse and never hears a sound.

He went along carefully. On his hands and knees. The tunnel had been carved from clay and traveled in a westerly direction. The floor was compacted. Every twenty feet or so a lantern. Two-by-fours braced the walls and ceiling. Martin crawled along in the muted yellow light. He'd reach a place where no light fell, and then would come the next amber glow. He tried the flashlight at first, but he could see well enough without it. It only gave away location. He crawled past the third light and looked back in the direction of the shed. He nodded to himself. That this was crazy. Someone could shoot him or the ceiling give way. He'd get stuck down here and no way to call out. The sheriff crouched there a moment. He backhanded the sweat from his forehead and continued to crawl.

He reached a bend. Gradual at first. Then a right angle. Another. The tunnel began to slope, running slightly diagonal. It occurred to Martin he was turning in the direction of the shed. He stopped. Backed a few feet. He reached up and smoothed his hand across the ceiling. It crumbled against his palm. Martin looked behind him. He pressed himself against the floor and looked up ahead. He crawled forward ten feet. Twelve. It seemed the tunnel was begin-

ning to widen. There was a cluster of lanterns, or at least several
lights. He went several more feet and he could see it now. Some
kind of hollow. He blinked once or twice, stopped again, and lay
there. He wiped the sweat away and rose to a crouch.

It was a chamber. A space in the earth. Like a nightmare or
vision. Martin wondered how far down. He couldn't imagine what
it took to build. You'd dig these holes as a kid, five, six feet. Like as
not, you'd strike sandstone and have to quit. You'd go down a little
and hit clay. It was one of the things people said about Oklahoma,
how hard the soil was, how hard it was to dig. Even in a region of
heavy topsoil, it would still have been a feat. The clay would have
helped it. Made the structure sturdier, less likely to cave.

Martin thought about that. He gripped his pistol tighter and
crawled into the room.

It was roughly circular, maybe twenty feet from wall to wall.
You'd have to crouch in order to stand. There were two-by-twelves
cut to length and propped against sections of plywood on the ceiling. There were pillows along the walls. Thermal blankets and
quilts. Suspended from the sections of plywood, five lanterns, six.
The lamps hung from pieces of twine. Martin knelt there, letting
his eyes adjust. On the far side of the room, a perfectly round hole
had been cut in the floor. Directly above it, another hole of the
same diameter, carved in the ceiling like a flue. The sheriff glanced
about. Motes swirled in the lantern light. He came several feet
ahead. He got his legs under him, began to stand, and just then a
shadow jerked to his left. He started to turn toward it, but there
was a flash behind his eyes and a sharp pain in his temple. Martin
pitched forward, and when he came to himself, the man was on top
of him.

The sheriff lay on his back. His vision blurred. The man who
now straddled him was all beard and bare skin. Filthy. His hair a
terra-cotta red. Martin flailed and tried to push him away, but the

man was too strong. He pinned the sheriff, fed him a right hand. He fed another, the blows landing on Martin's eyebrow, his cheek. Martin fetched at the man's wrists. He fetched for his gun. The pistol had been knocked somewhere he couldn't see. He had a pair of cuffs in a pouch on his belt, jammed now in the small of his back. He had an expandable baton in a holster and a knife clipped to his pocket. He wanted the knife. He tried to snake a hand down to reach it and ate another fist.

This one was harder and the room went dark. Then it lightened. The sheriff scrambled. He bucked the man and tried to push him to the wall. The man was wearing trousers, nothing else. Barefoot. His body smeared various colors. He had his legs hooked around the sheriff and he torqued his body and took Martin's back. Martin pushed away and the two of them rolled and the man ended up, somehow, atop the sheriff, straddling him once more, punching. He landed a couple of shots, he landed an elbow, and then he anchored his forearm across Martin's throat and began pressing down. The sheriff spat and sputtered. He could feel his wind cutting off and he could feel the blood flow cutting. He saw spots and above him the man's eyes were two sockets of black. His lips parted and his teeth clenched together. Martin could feel himself passing. He'd heard about these experiences, what people thought. He'd never believed it. How you'd have time to think. Or that time would pause to let you.

But this was exactly what it did. It crept slower and slower and then seemed to stop. The first thing he thought was that he would die in this place and the second was that he'd never be found. Just like his brother, his body lost, and Martin thought what Deborah would do about that, what she would tell their boy. He tried to picture her saying this, tried to picture her face, and there was such sadness to it, Martin couldn't even say. Other things crowded in, other sensations, but mostly a panic, all he'd left undone. Things unanswered, things left unsaid, information he needed and would never retrieve. The sheriff couldn't take that. It was like an iron on his chest. His hands clawed at fabric. His breathing constricted. His vision began tunneling and he reached out, caught the corner of the man's mouth, inserted his thumb in it, and fishhooked him all the way to the ear. There was a sound like ripping carpet.

The man let go immediately. He stumbled back. The skin was torn in a jagged line across his cheek, the lower part of his face hanging, his mouth jerked in a hideous mask. He grabbed at it, gaped at his palm, and when he did this, Martin pushed him several feet and fetched out his knife. He unfolded the blade and held it before him, swiping through the air, gasping breaths now, coughing. Light winked off the tongue of steel and the man seemed to see it. Martin tried to say something, warn him, back him farther, but he hadn't recovered his voice. He came onto both knees and that was when he saw. His revolver lying on the floor not three feet away. About equal distance between him and the man.

Martin looked at the weapon and then at the form crouching across from him, one hand still clutching his face. The sheriff was sucking air, holding the knife out like a caution. The man didn't move. He stood there watching. Martin couldn't tell if he saw the pistol or he didn't. He was scared to look again, afraid it would make the man notice.

They stayed frozen like that.

Then the man did notice. You could see it in his eyes.

The sheriff drew a breath and prepared himself to leap for it. That was when the man came suddenly forward and seized the knife from his grasp.

It happened just like that. It was in the sheriff's hand and then it wasn't. In one motion he trapped Martin's wrist and turned it, pushing out the blade. Martin retreated a step and the man bent and came at him. The knife was in his grip now and he feinted with a high slash and then sank the blade into the sheriff's left thigh. Martin groaned. He fetched at his leg. The man had one hand on the knife, trying to sink it deeper, and Martin was trying to hold it still. He looked down and saw the blood welling, the man with one hand gripping the handle and the other pressed against the spine of the blade. Every time it moved there was a pain like electricity. They crouched like that, clenched, bent as though straining together to pick something up. Pieces of spittle collected on the sheriff's face, speckles of blood. The sheriff panted. Then he collapsed, fell away from the man, and the blade came free. He was all dead weight, falling, and then he was scurrying crabwise across the floor. He was pushing with his hands and his feet and he sat down hard on something. The man was coming back in on him when the sheriff reached beneath him and retrieved the gun. He slapped the barrel against his knee to knock the dirt out of it and trained the weapon on the man's chest.

The man stopped cold. He backed a few feet. Then he backed a few more. The silence in the chamber was like the silence of a tomb. The sheriff struggled to his knees. There was blood running down in his boot and he could feel it filling that hollow place in his arch. In interrogation, they'd get everything out. Learn about Parks. Learn the boy's location. Martin could sleep finally, put it all to rest. He steadied his hands on the pistol and looked down its sights. Between them, he could see the man clearly for the first time, eyes staring back at him like black buttons in dough.

Martin cocked the hammer.

"Hickson," he said.

There was no reaction. He seemed unfamiliar with the name. Martin moved a few inches closer. Something was settling down inside him, even with all the blood. Relief, partly, but it was more than just that. There was a sense the world was working, its contours coming straight, and he knew, whatever the circumstances, Hickson, now, was his.

"There," rasped the sheriff, "get on the ground."

The man responded by lifting his palms. The left side of his face hung loose, the tear extending up his cheek in half a savage grin.

"Get on the ground," repeated Martin. "Interlace your fingers."

The man didn't. He curled his arms to his chest instead. He curled his arms to his chest, crossed and composed them, one atop the other. He glanced at Martin and then he closed his eyes. Martin was about to repeat his instructions when the man dropped suddenly backward, tucking himself, forehead to knees. Martin knelt there, watching Hickson fall, mute, serene, as though plunging into waves. Hard as the floor was, Martin thought he'd break his back.

The man didn't break anything. He didn't strike the floor. He fell like this away from Martin, past shadow and clay. The light strobed his body a final time and then he vanished down the hole.

The sheriff dove to reach for him, but he was already gone.

EPILOGUE

She went into labor the next week. Martin was driving back from a visit with the county commissioner, and he'd just made the city limits when the call came through.

"Sheriff," Nita told him, "it's time," and Martin flipped on his siren and lights.

When he got to the hospital, Lem was already waiting. Deborah was in delivery, and Martin sat beside his deputy, getting reports from the nurse. He'd seen, on television, husbands who went into the room with their wives, but this was Perser Memorial, and that didn't happen here. He sat with head drooped and knees bouncing. He glanced up at one point and looked at Lem. The man backhanded him in the arm.

"Both of us here," he said. "Probably come a crime spree."

Martin nodded. He looked at the floor.

He didn't have long to wait. The doctor came through the double doors, pulling off his gloves.

"Congratulations," he told the sheriff. "It's a girl."

Martin sat, staring.

Beside him, Lemming released a laugh.

They ushered him back to the room. It smelled of iodine and iron. On the bed, Deborah lay with hair damp and her face bone-white. She held, in her arms, their daughter. So small. They'd just cut the cord and swaddled her and her skin was a bright shade of red. Martin limped up, leaned his cane against the bedside, and placed his hand on Deborah's shoulder. He looked down at the silent form, his likeness. The baby shivered, then opened her eyes.

Deborah looked up at him.

"Janice," she told him. "Janice Therese."

"Yes," said Martin.

And Janice it was.

The doctors explained about misreading the sonogram. They xeroxed an article from the *Journal of Modern Medicine.* An obstetrician and two gynecologists talked to them and gestured. It never, to Martin, made any sense. Somehow, Martin didn't need it to. Evenings, he'd come home, and they'd be there in one of the recliners, rocking. She sang to her. She sang "Wildwood Flower," and "Babes in the Woods," and another song she didn't know the words to and just hummed. Sometimes, in the middle of a chorus, she'd transfer Janice to Martin's arms, and he would gather his daughter against his chest and gently palm the back of her head. She never seemed to cry. Deborah would sing, and Martin would rock, and Janice would look up at him, blue eyes blinking. She'd stare straight into him and smile.

It was spring, and then it was summer. The county brought in backhoes to the house on Scrimshaw Lane. They tore down the fence and moved their equipment into Hickson's backyard. They removed the shed and began digging. They went down, thirty feet, forty, found what the foreman called the entrance to a well, began to try and recover bodies. Hickson's body. Perhaps even the boy. They didn't find anything, and Martin drove out twice a day and urged them to keep digging. The man operating the backhoe would stare at him a moment and then lower the machine's metal claw.

Then came the day Martin drove to the addition and saw a pickup pulled into Hickson's driveway with *Malcoz Petroleum* lettered across its doors. He parked, went around the side yard, and found men standing by the pit with clipboards, mumbling.

They sank the first shaft within the week. A derrick went up, right in the middle of the housing addition, and neighbors complained constantly about the noise. Martin and Lemming took calls of grievance, and then, the next Monday, the *Perser Chronicle* printed the story.

Malcoz Petroleum, in concert with another firm, had discovered a new formation. It was deep, deeper than the wells that had been drilled in the thirties. They said oil had seeped in from other formations, pooled beneath the suburb just north of the course. The find was mammoth. The largest since the Boom.

Folks in Perser said it was a godsend. The Corporation Commission said it would revitalize their economy. Give Perser a new beginning. Hickson Crider had no will, and his only living relative was a grandfather who was an Alzheimer's patient at the nursing home. His estate went to the county, the mineral rights as well. The city of Perser sold them to Malcoz, and the company began buying the homes in the subdivision, every house that sat on the hundred and sixty acres. One by one they were bulldozed, trees cleared, and Martin sat in his cruiser, watching the work. As soon as oil was mentioned, the notion of finding Hickson or the boy's body was dismissed as an impossibility, and the sheriff brought up the issue to be met only with stares. The mayor took the sheriff aside at a town meeting and explained how those folk were gone; they weren't coming back. It was suggested to Martin that if he hoped for reelection, he might drop the issue entirely.

He caught Enoch coming out of his building one evening. If

the man was surprised to see him, he didn't show it. The sheriff told him of the problems they'd had retrieving the bodies. He said he knew Enoch's firm had purchased the subdivision, that more drilling would commence. He begged the man to give them time.

Enoch stood there. He wouldn't give an answer. He wouldn't look away.

Martin studied him a moment and cleared his throat. He looked behind him at the cars going down Main and then glanced over at the post office. He asked him was it just about the money.

Enoch shook his head.

"It is not what I wanted," he told the sheriff. "It is not the way the story goes."

Then he turned and started walking.

Martin watched him out of sight.

By the end of summer the subdivision was leveled, and there were eight wells in its place, gravel roads, rows of holding tanks and disposal units. You could stand on the property line between the golf course and the former addition, and it looked like something from science fiction. On one side, greens, the grass immaculate. On the other, cracked clay and pumpjacks and dark patches where the oil had run. The Malcoz Estate standing in the midst of this waste-land like a fortress at the edge of the world. There were always men working, but they were brought in from out of state, mostly, and very few of Perser's citizens were given actual jobs. Property values around the golf course plummeted, more folks moved away. In two years the town had lost another thousand residents. Martin would study the figures on reports sent to them by the Senate. He'd show Lemming and the man would shake his head.

Martin went out, one evening, to speak with J.T.'s grandmother, his aunt. He pulled into the drive and went up the steps. He later learned the family had relocated. Shreveport, Louisiana. The house sat as they had left it. Shuttered. Locked. Much of the furniture left behind and draped with sheets. It was on Indian land and the tribe would reassign as they saw fit. Martin stood there. He went around to the back, let himself in through the cellar, came up into the kitchen from the basement stairs. He walked about from room to room. Silent. A smell of must. The electricity had been turned off and the only noise was the sound of the floorboards creaking beneath his weight.

He walked into the living room. He walked into the den. He stood, looking around. The house reminded him of a mausoleum. He couldn't envision the boy having lived there at all.

He walked back into the living room and then up the carpeted steps to the second story. There were pale rectangles along the cedar-paneled walls where pictures had hung. He went down the hallway to the grandmother's room and the bed was bare of its blankets and mattress. Other than this, everything as it had been. Martin walked over and parted the shades and looked out the window, down to his car. Then he walked back down the hallway and opened the door to the boy's room. Stepped inside.

The mattress and pillow remained on the bed. The pillowcase and sheets. The quilt had been removed, but the walls were still papered with the boy's clippings. The row of shoes lined before the dresser. Martin went over and opened the drawer. A few pairs of jeans. A small stack of shirts. There was a bandanna that had been folded into a headband. He could tell it hadn't been washed. Martin lifted it from the drawer, stood there and held it. He brought it to his nostrils. Then he went over and sat on the bed. He began speaking, though no one was there. It felt like he could do that. Like a visit, somehow, to an altar or shrine.

The sheriff talked for a long time. He talked of what had disturbed him, what, he thought, no longer would. He talked about what he'd learned down there, how he'd let go. There were people, he said, who required his attention, living people, present. He wanted to keep searching, but he was sorry, and things now were different. There were some things, he said, beyond understanding. There were things absolutely beyond his control.

When he finished, he wiped his face on his shirtsleeve and stood to his feet. He looked around at the clippings, the golfers and equipment and clothing and greens. Then he walked over, opened the dresser, and put back the bandanna. He closed the drawer, went to the door, and then he went back. He opened the drawer and fetched the bandanna and placed it in his pocket. Then he left the room and went down the stairs.

He returned to the house several times. The house was always the same. A little staler. A bit more decayed. He'd walk up to the boy's room and just sit. It was comforting, somehow. A place he could dream. One evening, he arrived and found a family unloading from a U-Haul trailer. Martin pulled the cruiser around the circle and a man coming down the steps studied him with a puzzled look. Martin lifted a hand, made the loop, and went back down the drive.

Janice was a year old. Then she was two. The sheriff would walk down sometimes after dinner, pick a path through the oak grove, and stand by the pond. There were no lights in the country and on clearer nights you'd look up and the sky was filled with stars. Orion. The Dipper. Cassiopeia and other constellations Martin didn't know. He'd stand there, staring at all that. It was November and Deborah was pregnant once again. He'd have the bandanna in his left pocket. He'd slip his hand down and rub it between his thumb and forefinger, think about the boy, the way he imagined him. He was older now, taller. He'd gone back to high school in Martin's thoughts, graduated. He'd been accepted at the University of Oklahoma on an athletic scholarship and had begun to make himself a name. His short game kept getting better and better. People all over would talk of his drive. Martin saw him in the PGA. He saw him on television. The Masters. He stood there in the starlight with the pond like a mirror giving back a vision of the sky, the sky doubled, countless reflections. He waited a few moments, going further into dream. He'd go a bit further the night that followed. The night after that. Then he nodded to himself and zipped his coat higher. He turned and walked back through the woods, up the path, up toward Deborah and Janice and the child they'd be having, the angles of lamplight spilling from his home.

ACKNOWLEDGMENTS

I would like to thank to my agent, Nat Sobel, and my editor, Jill Bialosky. Thanks also to Judith Weber. To Emily Russo and Adia Wright. To Paul Whitlatch and Adrienne Davich: of greater assistance than I can even say. Love always to my brother, Clint. To Stephen Morrison and Adam Schnier. This novel is inscribed to my grandfather and dedicated to Lance Corporal Scott Sparks (U.S.M.C. ret.).